A PENGUIN SPECIAL

HEROIN: CHASING THE DRAGON

Justine Picardie was born in 1961 in London and educated at schools in London, Oxford and Cardiff. She took a degree in English at Cambridge University, and then a postgraduate diploma in journalism at City University. She has worked as a freelance journalist for the *New Statesman*, and joined the *Sunday Times* in 1983.

Dorothy Wade was born in 1959, and educated in Glasgow and at St Andrew's University. From 1980 to 1982 she taught English in a school in Nigeria, and wrote on education in Nigeria for *The Times Educational Supplement*. She took a postgraduate diploma in journalism at City University and in 1983 she joined the *Sunday Times* as a journalist.

HEROIN
Chasing the Dragon

JUSTINE PICARDIE

DOROTHY WADE

PENGUIN BOOKS

Penguin Books Ltd, Harmondsworth, Middlesex, England
Viking Penguin Inc., 40 West 23rd Street, New York, New York 10010, U.S.A.
Penguin Books Australia Ltd, Ringwood, Victoria, Australia
Penguin Books Canada Ltd, 2801 John Street, Markham, Ontario, Canada L3R 1B4
Penguin Books (N.Z.) Ltd, 182-190 Wairau Road, Auckland 10, New Zealand

First published 1985

Made and printed in Great Britain by
Richard Clay (The Chaucer Press) Ltd, Bungay, Suffolk
Filmset in Monophoto Photina by
Northumberland Press Ltd, Gateshead, Tyne and Wear

Introduction

David started using heroin when he was 15, along with most of his friends that lived on the council estates off the Old Kent Road in south London. He was an addict by the age of 16, stealing to pay for the £5 'ching bags' of heroin, and ended up in a detention centre. Unable to find a job when he got out, he gradually drifted back to his old friends and his old heroin habit.

Hetty left boarding school when she was 17, and moved to London, where she found an abundant supply of heroin amongst her social circle. She used to buy heroin from insurance underwriters in the City, who were dealing to support their own habits. Hetty was only able to give up heroin after a seven-month stay in an expensive private clinic.

Jim is a 40-year-old businessman, with a red Ferrari and a taste for skiing, hang-gliding, and windsurfing. He was introduced to a new pastime – smoking heroin – by some of his younger colleagues at his thriving employment agency. Within eighteen months, the company had collapsed as a result of his expensive and debilitating habit.

These three people are all victims of the heroin epidemic that is sweeping the country. The drug is cheaper now than ever before, and flooding into Britain in enormous quantities.

Heroin is now freely available in most towns and cities throughout the country. The number of addicts is soaring and includes people from many different backgrounds. It is used for any number of reasons – unemployment and bad housing, boredom, loneliness or insecurity – and perhaps just because it is a fashionable thing to do. 'Chasing the Dragon', which involves heating heroin and inhaling the fumes, has caught on as a new craze – and is often accompanied by the myth that using heroin in this way is not addictive. But the warm, cocooning comfort that heroin offers can be very seductive – and extremely difficult to give up.

The government was, at first, slow to read the warning signs and reluctant to devote scarce resources to helping drug addicts. Patrick Jenkin, secretary of state at the Department of Health and Social Security, told a meeting held in 1980 at a rehabilitation centre for addicts that although no one could question the value of customs' surveillance or the police campaign against traffickers: 'It must be very evident to those in this hall that the same cannot always be said about research or still more about the efforts to rehabilitate drug abusers.'

Now, at least, the government has recognized that the problem of heroin addiction has to be tackled. It has launched its new anti-heroin strategy, recruiting more customs officers and pledging £1 million to a United Nations fund to help the Pakistani government to reduce the opium crop. The police have declared their intention to crack down on big dealers, instead of individual addicts. Grants of £10 million have been promised for health authorities and voluntary agencies to provide new advice and treatment centres, and another £2 million for an advertising campaign to warn children and parents of the dangers of heroin.

But customs officers are still thinly stretched along the coastline, and in practice the police carry on hauling in the small fry while most of the big dealers carry on trading. Treatment facilities are overwhelmed, and most heroin addicts have to find a cure by themselves. Britain's experience of heroin up till the late 1970s has not prepared us for the present crisis. The bedrock of our drugs policy is the network of hospital treatment-centres clustered largely around London and set up for an estimated 1200 addicts in 1968. Our 'medical model' of drugs control seems sadly inadequate when faced with the thousands of kilos of heroin reaching us by air, land and sea, eagerly awaited by Britain's thousands of heroin users, young and old. Equally the history of opium addiction in other countries suggests that neither draconian prohibition nor legalization is the correct solution for a crisis of this magnitude. As Bing Spear, the Chief Inspector of the Home Office Drugs Branch, says,

'The heroin problem of the 1960s was seen as a challenge to the practice of medicine; the problem of the 1980s is very much a challenge to the whole community.'

Whether the government has understood this is open to doubt. For the addicts and their families with no hope of finding help, the government has not moved much further on from the rhetoric of Home Secretary Leon Brittan's speech to the London Diplomatic Association in December 1983: 'Drug abuse is a disease from which no country and no section of modern society seems immune. It brings ruthless, hardened criminals and weak, self-indulgent users together in a combination which is potentially lethal for good order and civilized values. It requires cooperation between Governments, law-enforcement agencies, professionals, schools and families. The rewards are great if we succeed – and the price of ultimate failure unthinkable.'

Acknowledgements

This book would have been impossible without the help of the dozens of addicts, parents, doctors and policemen who wrote to us and talked to us about their experiences.

We would like to thank Detective Chief Superintendent Roy Penrose, of the Metropolitan Police Drug Squad, and Detective Superintendent Derek Olley, who worked at the Central Drugs Intelligence Unit until July 1985. The Standing Conference on Drugs Abuse (SCODA) and treatment centres have given freely of their valuable time and help.

We would like to thank the Institute for the Study of Drug Dependence for the use of their library. Two books in particular were invaluable sources for the chapter on the history of opiate use: *Opium and the People* by Virginia Berridge and Griffith Edwards; and *The Forbidden Game* by Brian Inglis.

We would like to thank the editor of the *Sunday Times*, Andrew Neil, for the time and resources he has given us to work on the book, and the encouragement for the original series of articles on heroin. All this would have been impossible without Paul Eddy and Sara Walden, who are both friends and colleagues.

Bibliography

Virginia Berridge and Griffith Edwards, *Opium and the People: Opiate Use in Nineteenth Century England*, Allen Lane/St Martin's Press, 1981.

Brian Inglis, *The Forbidden Game: A Social History of Drugs*, Hodder and Stoughton, 1981.

H. B. Spear, *British Experience in the Management of Opiate Dependence*, MTP Press Limited, 1982.

Kenneth Leech, *Keep the Faith Baby: A Close-up of London's Dropouts*, London SPCK, 1973.

Barry Cox, John Shirley, Martin Short, *The Fall of Scotland Yard*, Penguin, 1977.

Gerry V. Stimson and Edna Oppenheimer, *Heroin Addiction: Treatment and Control in Britain*, Tavistock Publications, 1982.

Treatment and Rehabilitation, Report of the Advisory Council on the Misuse of Drugs, HMSO, 1982.

Arnold S. Trebach, *The Heroin Solution*, Yale University Press, 1982.

H. B. Spear, 'The Growth of Heroin Addiction in the United Kingdom', *British Journal of Addiction*, 1969.

[1] A cash crop

By the beginning of 1984, the wholesale supply of heroin was a fact of life in towns and cities throughout Britain. Parents, doctors, policemen, customs officers and MPs had to admit that the problem was reaching alarming proportions. David Mellor, the Home Office minister who had been put at the head of a new working group on illegal drugs, was openly expressing concern by the summer: 'What is most worrying is the evidence that drug abuse has moved away from being a minority cult. No one can honestly say that they haven't got a drugs problem in their part of the country now.'

The government seemed powerless to stop the flood of cheap, high-quality heroin that was pouring into the country. By the time it reached the street, it cost less than £60 a gram – half what it cost (in real terms) at the end of the 1970s. And despite the record 300 kilos of heroin seized by customs and police in 1984, the price showed no sign of being forced up – and the purity of the drug stayed high. Officers privately admitted that they were stopping less than 10 per cent of the heroin being imported into Britain. Some even guessed that seizures were only 1 per cent of the total amount cascading into the country.

The marketing of the drug was – *and still is* – extremely efficient, reflecting the increasing involvement of British professional criminals, who a few years ago would have frowned at any suggestion of trading in heroin. Although most of the small dealers were – *and are* – addicts, financing their own habits, the non-using top-level traffickers have brought a new, smooth-running slickness to the business.

The reason for this criminal involvement is simple – the profits to be made are enormous. Detective Superintendent Derek Olley, of the Central Drugs Intelligence Unit at Scotland Yard, describes heroin trafficking as 'the most profitable form of criminality known to mankind. A kilo of heroin plus air-fares and overheads comes to around £5000 in Pakistan. The moment your courier sets foot in the UK, the same kilo is worth around £25–£30,000. By the time it reaches the streets, it will be worth about £100,000 ... You don't need to be a mathematical genius to work out there's a handsome profit to be made.'

Olley points out that if one takes the very conservative estimate of 30,000 regular users taking one fifth of a gram every day – or 75 grams annually – that adds up to 2250 kilos of heroin a year coming into the country. The profits made on that by the top men would be over £45 million, and the total amount generated by the 2250 kilos as it moved down the chain of dealers to the street, £112.5 million. The real sums are likely to be much larger than these, as the number of addicts is closer to 50–60,000, many of whom use a gram of heroin a day.

As Lord Justice Lane told the annual Judges' Dinner in July 1984, 'the criminal heavies – the first-division crooks – are finding that dealing in heroin is a safer and easier source of income than holding up the high street bank.' According to Derek Olley, 'it knocks the most successful robbery, the Brinks-Mat bullion job, into a cocked hat ... It's more profitable, and the risk factor is far less than robbing a bank, when the villain has to carry a shooter, and actually get out there and do the job. A drugs trafficker can pay someone else to do the dirty work for him. The big villains just place the order for heroin, finance it, and let someone else organize the couriers.'

The source of these vast profits is the opium poppy. Usually planted in the autumn, the poppy does best in a warm, not too humid climate. It grows to about three feet tall on a thin stalk, and produces several blossoms and egg-sized seed-pods. About two weeks after the blossoms fall, the pods are lanced by hand and the white, raw opium oozes out and forms a gum. The gum is collected by scraping the pods, and is then allowed to harden, and either powdered or moulded into bricks. Morphine base is chemically extracted from opium, and is then converted into heroin.

Most of the heroin that is coming into this country is manufactured from poppies grown in South-West Asia. The heart of the opium-producing area there is in the 'Golden Crescent', stretching from Pakistan's North-West Frontier Province across Afghanistan to Iran. It is a largely autonomous tribal region, and opium tends to be the only cash crop – and ideal for the area. As one senior British customs investigator admitted after seeing the region: 'If you were to feed all the climactic facts about the area into a computer, to find out the best crop to grow there, the answer would be the opium poppy.'

Each farmer in the area would probably grow just over an acre of poppies, and get seven kilos of opium per acre. Many of these tribal farmers are the Pathans, a fiercely independent people, and renowned traders of electrical goods, guns, opium, heroin and cannabis. A rather stunned customs officer commented on his return from the North-West Frontier: 'The main commodity for sale is heroin – and the very best modern weapons and televisions and stereo equipment I've ever seen. The shiny technology is in complete contrast to the rugged stone houses ... but the people who live there are immensely capable and hard-talking businessmen.'

The area is extremely difficult to control, and although the Pakistani authorities have had some success in reducing the amount of opium grown, poppy farming flourishes just across the border in Afghanistan. So with a plentiful supply of the raw material, heroin production continues to flourish in the North-West Frontier Province – and whenever the threat of action by the Pakistani government looms, the traffickers merely move their activities to even more isolated areas, or hop across the border. There appear to be no real effective controls on either side of the line between Pakistan and Afghanistan. 'It's like trying to police the South Armagh border,' commented one customs official – 'only this no-man's land is a hundred times bigger.' And South Armagh does not depend on a cash crop that is vital for a war – unlike this frontier, which pays for the guns to fight the Soviets on the other side with opium, and harvests the poppy with the cheap labour provided by Afghan refugees.

South-West Asia has not always been the major source of heroin for this country. During the early and mid-Seventies, Britain was supplied by South-East Asian heroin from the notorious Golden Triangle of Burma, Laos and Thailand.

The drug was imported on a fairly small scale, coming in via Hong Kong to London's Chinese community, and circulating around Piccadilly Circus. With many of the US troops in Vietnam using heroin regularly, there was a sufficiently large local market to absorb most of the production of the Golden Triangle. But at the end of the Vietnam war, new markets were needed to consume the 750–1000 tonnes of opium produced every year by the hill tribes of the Triangle, overseen by their local warlords. Heroin began to move westward, under the control of the Triads and other gangs. But it was Amsterdam, rather than London, that emerged as the drug capital of Europe, with its comparatively liberal drug laws, and impenetrable Chinese community providing the hub of an efficient trafficking network.

By the late 1970s supplies of heroin from the Golden Triangle fell away, and the price rose dramatically, after bad weather and drought caused the low opium harvests of 1978–79. The going rate for one kilo of heroin on the Thai/Burmese border went up from 2000 US dollars in January 1979 to 7500 dollars in June 1980.

At the same time bumper crops in Pakistan, Afghanistan and Iran – the result of good weather and increased planting – pushed South-West Asian heroin to the forefront of the market. In 1979, about 1600 metric tonnes of opium were grown there – twice as much as the normal supply.

There was another change in production patterns that has had an impact on the burgeoning heroin market. Increased production in South-West Asia is not the only reason for the falling cost of heroin – the drug is now being refined close to the poppy fields, bringing down the price of transportation between farming areas and laboratories.

In the old days, the 'French Connection' in its heyday of the 1950s and 1960s, was the main supplier of illicit heroin to the

United States. At that time, what was mainly Turkish opium was turned into morphine base in Turkey, Syria or the Lebanon, and then shipped to France for conversion into heroin, with a hefty mark-up of the price at every stage. When the French Connection was wrecked in the early Seventies, the morphine-base chemists were encouraged to take their skills one step further – and by 1977 their beige-coloured heroin was beginning to appear on the market.

By 1979, heroin laboratories had been set up in Syria, Lebanon, Pakistan, Iran, Turkey and Afghanistan – with a cluster in the Kurdish homelands straddling the borders of Turkey, Syria and Iran. Although the heroin produced was initially crude, it has reached 80 per cent purity in the 1980s. Even after dilution by dealers, heroin can be bought on the streets of this country with a purity of 50 per cent – unlike America, where it is often less than 5 per cent pure.

The crackdown by Ayatollah Khomeini after his takeover in Iran in 1979 did nothing to improve the situation, for the chemists he pushed out of the country merely took their skills elsewhere, proving to be skilled tutors to the novice producers on the north-western frontier.

All this led to a dramatic fall in prices all along the chain, from the cost of the raw-opium base to the final product of heroin. The farmers who grow the poppy in the north-western frontier area would have been paid about £22 a kilo for opium early in 1980 – a fall from about £100 a kilo before the previous year's surplus crop glutted the market.

Another indication of the massive fall in price is that one kilo of heroin, purchased in 1984 on the north-western frontier for £3–4000, might have cost as much as £50,000 from a laboratory in Marseilles in 1980. But local profits are still high enough to make the heroin business an attractive one. According to US Drug Enforcement Administration intelligence, after the glut in the harvests that brought in this decade, 'the sharp decline in prices paid for opium during 1982 and 1983 may have further spurred Pakistani involvement in heroin production. By controlling both opium processing and final heroin production, the Pakistani trafficker more than made up the profit lost by reduced opium prices.'

As a result of this efficient, cost-effective system, the availability of heroin in this country is reflected in the relentless rise in the number of addicts. As Leon Brittan, the Home Secretary, told the London Diplomatic Association in December 1983: 'Let us be clear. The effects of that trend will be with us not for months, but for years. No matter how vigorous the action we take to stem the flow from abroad and control availability at home, the price will continue to be paid in addiction and associated crime for some time to come.'

It has taken a long time for heroin to emerge as the social blight it is known as today. It was invented almost by chance in 1874, at St Mary's Hospital in London by a British chemist who was performing a series of experiments on morphine, and popularized by a German pharmacologist as a painkiller and cure-all. For thousands of years people had relied on opium to cure every imaginable ill, but in the late nineteenth century its popularity waned as opium addiction became a serious social problem.

Opium has been eaten, drunk and smoked in many countries both for its medical and pleasure-giving properties. The Sumerians in 4000 BC called the opium poppy 'plant of joy'. The juice of the poppy is referred to on Assyrian medical tablets from the seventh century BC. As the growth of 'papaver somniferum', the white opium poppy, spread from Mesopotamia to Egypt to Greece, it occupied a central place in Roman, Greek and Arabic medicine. But descriptions by ancient medical experts show that both the toxic and euphoric effects of opium were well-known. Homer's Odyssey refers to a drug dissolved in wine which had the power to bring 'forgetfulness of evil'.

In England, opium was used from medieval times, mainly for narcotic purposes. Its soporific qualities are mentioned by Chaucer in *The Canterbury Tales* and by Shakespeare in *Othello*. In the mid-fourteenth century, opium-based medicines were used as anaesthetics as well as sleeping-potions. In the 1660s, Thomas Sydenham, the English physician who mixed opium with alcohol to produce laudanum, the widely-used Victorian 'cure-all', said of it: 'Among the remedies which it has pleased Almighty God to give to man to relieve his sufferings none is so universal and efficacious as opium.'

It is strange to contrast reports from travellers about opium use in the East with early English use of opium as a 'sedative'. Travellers in the Middle East and India wrote again and again of Indian warriors and wrestlers who took opium to perform feats of prodigious strength and to make them fearless and daring in war. Peasants chewed the leaf, apparently with little ill effect, much as Bolivian and Peruvian workers chew the coca leaf today, to help them endure arduous physical labour.

Virginia Berridge and Griffith Edwards, in their book *Opium and the People*, say that the stimulant and addictive effects of the drug were known in England at least from the beginning of the eighteenth century but were rarely admitted because of 'cultural prejudices and literary convention'. But there are several rare references to opium addiction in the eighteenth century. Thomas Shadwell, the Restoration dramatist and subject of 'MacFlecknoe', a vicious satiric poem by Dryden, was known to be an opium addict. Dr John Jones' book, *Mysteries of Opium Revealed*, published in 1700, treats the question of addiction. But though he mentions the drug's drawbacks, he emphasizes the pleasures to be derived from it: 'It has been compared to a permanent gentle degree of that pleasure which modesty forbids the name of . . .'

So at the beginning of the nineteenth century in England, opium was regarded by doctors and ordinary people as a useful and pleasant cure for many disorders. There were a handful of addicts who were largely treated by society as harmless but foolish figures of fun. Throughout that century, however, attitudes were to harden as the dangers of the drug were recognized, as its use spread among all classes of society, and addiction, particularly, was highlighted as a medical problem. The anti-opium movement which developed in Victorian times is comparable to the waves of anti-heroin hysteria which the twentieth century has witnessed. How did it come about?

Many people have heard of Coleridge writing his long visionary poem 'Kubla Khan' under the influence of opium or of Thomas De Quincey's *Confessions of an Opium Eater*. The popular image is of opium as the drug of a creative élite of Romantic poets and artists. Certainly there is a long list of nineteenth-century writers who took opium at various periods in their lives.

Wilkie Collins, who first took opium for rheumatic complaints and then carried a silver flask of it for the rest of his life, wrote *The Moonstone* under its influence. Walter Scott was taking it when he wrote *The Bride of Lammermoor*. Elizabeth Barrett Browning was a 'well-balanced addict' who took opium regularly – rather like long-term heroin addicts today who are maintained on regular doses of opiates. Francis Thompson who confessed to trying opium after reading De Quincey was more unfortunate – he descended into destitution, a secret addict.

But there was also a more common middle-class problem of opium addicts who were given opium for illness or who took it themselves for some minor ailment. There are many nineteenth-century examples of doctors, preachers, politicians and soldiers who were under its thrall. Clive of India died in a fit, probably after overdosing, William Wilberforce took it for many years, and George Harley, professor of practical physiology at University College Hospital, had to wean himself off morphia. Even George IV was given opiates – to counteract excessive drinking!

More disturbing for the authorities in the nineteenth century was the widespread use of opium by ordinary working-class men, women and children. Most of this opium came from Turkey, although small amounts were cultivated at home. The main London dealers were the Levant Company and the opium was sold by open auction at Garraway's Coffee House near the Royal Exchange to a wide range of drug wholesalers and apothecaries.

Opium was freely available to anyone who wanted to buy it. It was sold by qualified pharmacists and by tailors, bakers and basket-makers – in chemists' shops, grocers' shops and small corner-shops. In the 1850s there were between 16,000 and 26,000 known sellers of the drug and probably many more in back-street shops. They sold opium in all its forms – opium pills, opiate lozenges, opiate plaster, opiate enema, opium liniment, vinegar of opium, wine of opium and tincture of opium – the popular alcohol mixture known as laudanum. Many of the medicines had friendly sounding names like Mrs Winslow's Soothing Syrup, Godfrey's Cordial – a children's opiate based on laudanum – and Battley's Sedative Solution, a mixture of opium, calcium, hydrate, alcohol, sherry and water.

Everyone had a bottle of laudanum at home in the nineteenth century. It was used to cure all ills, from coughs, whooping cough, earache, toothache and headaches to fatigue, depression and hang-overs. Although the myth of the miracle drug continued well into the century, many people died from accidental overdoses of opium. Others became addicted.

A London doctor noticed that 'the poor' were among the greatest users of the drug: 'Persons who never think of narcotizing them-selves, anymore than they would by getting drunk; but who simply desire a relief from the pains of fatigue endured by an ill-fed, ill-housed body and a harassed mind.'

But by the late nineteenth century, the higher echelons of the medical profession began to get seriously worried about the problems of opium addiction. In their medical practice, they tried to replace opium by drugs such as quinine and bromide for lesser complaints and to restrict its use to certain serious illnesses. Groups of doctors began to specialize in addiction, which came to be seen as a disease and a social evil.

In 1868, a new Pharmacy Act included opium in a list of fifteen selected poisons to be sold only by qualified pharmacists. This encouraged the idea that opium should be under professional control, although loop-holes in the Act allowed some general sale of the drug and opium continued to be 'misused'. In any case many ordinary GPs continued to hand out opium freely to all comers.

The urgency of the problem was heightened by the use of a new drug – morphine – and a new way of using it – the needle. Morphine was isolated from opium at the beginning of the nineteenth century and entered accepted medical practice soon after. The 'hypodermic method' of injecting morphine, which was to become so popular with 'junkies' in the 1960s, was invented in 1845.

Although morphine is ten times as strong as opium, morphine injections were enthusiastically taken up by doctors for medical reasons and as a substitute for opium addicts – because the injections involved smaller amounts than opium eating. Sherlock Holmes' use of morphine to heighten his sensations during dreary spells of life when he had no mysteries to solve, is a well-known fictional case. But there were soon warnings that addiction was increasing because of morphine injections, and doctors began to write of a new disease called morphinism.

But morphine addiction was nothing compared to the threat that lay ahead from a newly invented but little-known drug – heroin. C. R. Alder-Wright invented heroin in London in 1874 during a series of experiments to combine morphine with various acids. He boiled a sample of morphine with acetic anhydride and produced a long list of compounds including diacetylmorphine or heroin. He left no indication of what he was trying to do and did not seem to recognize the importance of his discovery.

It was left to Heinrich Dreser, a German pharmacologist, to name and popularize the new drug in the late 1890s. He marketed the new substance under the name of heroin, from 'heroisch' meaning heroic or 'having a very powerful effect' (in the mediaeval medical sense). Dreser and his colleagues marvelled at the medical properties of heroin, as previous scientists had done at opium and morphine. They reported its powerful effect on coughs, chest pains, pneumonia and tuberculosis.

Heroin seemed to have advantages over the use of opium, with no unpleasant side-effects such as nausea, vomiting and constipation. Dreser also believed that it was not habit-forming. In the first few years of the twentieth century its medical use spread through many countries and Bayer Pharmaceutical Products advertised it in several languages as 'the sedative for coughs' along with another new drug, aspirin. Some doctors even used it to 'cure' morphine addiction. But heroin is two to six times as strong as morphine. It was not long before the addictive dangers of the new drug began to emerge.

[2] Trade routes

By 1920, doctors had radically changed their opinion of the miracle cure. 'Heroin used by a human being produces an unmoral savage ... who ... becomes cold-blooded and capable of committing any crime,' was one American doctor's chilling condemnation. The manufacture of heroin was banned in America in 1924 and thousands of doctors and pharmacists were charged under new laws brought in to crack down on the prescription of heroin to addicts.

British doctors resisted this hysterical approach. But the first jolt came when men returning from the First World War were found to be addicted to a range of drugs including heroin. In 1920, Captain Walter Elliot, an MP, said in Parliament that drug addiction in Britain was an 'evil, spreading I think more from the United States than from any other country'. Even at the beginning of the twentieth century, America already had perhaps 250,000 addicts.

The Home Office became convinced that doctors were giving addicts heroin and morphine to 'satisfy their craving' – not for medical treatment – and began to push for new laws to crack down on this practice. There was also international pressure – in 1912 the first international narcotics convention at the Hague insisted on new controls on the growing of opium and the manufacture of heroin and morphine. The 1920 Dangerous Drugs Act was introduced to bring the prescribing of drugs in Britain, mainly heroin and morphine, under control, and to restrict their export, import, manufacture, sale, distribution and possession. The police received lists of addicts and their doctors from the Home Office, which continued to push for an even harder line.

Quietly, the doctors thwarted the Home Office's aims. In 1926, Sir Humphrey Rolleston, President of the Royal College of Physicians, was chosen to head a committee, consisting mainly of doctors, on morphine and heroin addiction to advise the government on whether or not and in what circumstances to supply addicts with drugs. The 1920 Dangerous Drugs Act said that morphine and heroin should be used only for 'bona fide medical treatment'. The Rolleston Committee had to decide what 'bona fide medical treatment' meant.

Members of the committee went to America where drugs were already controlled by stringent laws and doctors who supplied opiates to addicts were liable to heavy sentences. The American experience set the committee against prohibition as a way to control drugs: a Dr Campbell reported, 'A vast clandestine commerce has grown up in that country ... the country is overrun by an army of pedlars who extort exorbitant prices from their helpless victims.'

Stringent laws did not seem to be necessary in Britain where, the Committee concluded, addiction to heroin and morphine was a rare occurrence which had declined since the 1920s Dangerous Drugs Act. There were probably 100–500 drug addicts at most.

They found that addiction to morphine was more common than to heroin, but heroin addiction was 'more disastrous in its physical effects' and more difficult to cure. There was a small 'underworld class' who used heroin as a 'snuff' for new and pleasurable sensations but most heroin addicts did jobs that involved considerable mental or nervous strain, usually in big cities. Addiction should be treated as an illness and not as a 'mere form of vicious indulgence'.

The Rolleston Committee finally recommended that doctors should be able to give morphine or heroin to patients who could not live 'a useful and fairly normal life' without them. It assumed that the new (1920) law would stamp out heroin addiction and that in any case addiction rarely resulted from 'mere curiosity or search for pleasurable sensation'. It paid little attention to illegitimate heroin because addicts were 'usually lacking in the determination and ingenuity' needed to obtain it. However they did establish medical tribunals to deal with doctors who prescribed carelessly.

The Rolleston advice proved to be the corner-stone of British policy on drugs, placing doctors' discretion at its very centre. Its tribunal system was never called on and the black market in heroin and morphine remained small between the wars. This was in sharp contrast to the United States where heroin addiction grew more and more serious.

In 1936, August Vollmer, a Californian chief of police, said, 'Stringent laws, spectacular police drives, vigorous prosecution and imprisonment of addicts and pedlars have proved not only useless and very expensive as means of correcting this evil but they are also unjustifiably and unbelievably cruel in their applications to the unfortunate drug victims ...' He went on to say that it was not a police problem, it was a medical problem. In Britain, the view that heroin addiction could best be handled by the medical profession was rarely dented until the 1980s.

While Home Office reports to the League of Nations in the 1930s said that drug addiction was rare, there were small but significant signs that heroin was becoming a drug of widespread misuse. The proportion of all known drug addicts using heroin grew from 5 per cent in 1935 to 19 per cent in 1952. Most of them had been given drugs for illness or were doctors and nurses.

But even before the Second World War there was a fashionable, artistic London set which was using illicit heroin, smuggled in from France. The ring-leaders of this circle probably started their pastime during trips to the Continent. Three members of the group would frequently travel to Paris to get London's heroin, until one of them was arrested at Dover in 1937 and the network broke up.

The next wave of heroin activity began in the early Fifties. In May 1951, a young man called Kevin Patrick Saunders broke into a hospital dispensary a few miles outside London and stole large amounts of morphine, heroin and cocaine. The police later discovered that he was dealing these drugs in the West End of London. Sixty-three addicts who turned up later in the Fifties were probably customers – or friends of customers – of Saunders. Many of them were musicians from the jazz-club world that was the centre of drug culture in the Fifties.

This episode was the first sign of an emerging heroin sub-culture in Britain. Heroin supplies in the Fifties and Sixties continued to depend on thefts from hospitals, chemist shops, warehouses and doctors' surgeries or on addicts selling off parts of their prescriptions – many could fool doctors into prescribing them more heroin than they needed. For the first time since Rolleston, there was a real problem with doctors who over-prescribed. But the law to deal with them was completely inadequate.

One particular case demonstrated this. It involved a doctor who gave seventy prescriptions of heroin to a heroin addict who he knew was another doctor's patient. He didn't consult the other doctor and gave most of the 'scrips' to the addict's girlfriend – herself an addict. A magistrate trying the case found that he had no powers to convict the doctor. The Brain Committee, set up in 1960 to overhaul drug controls, merely condemned bad prescribing but did nothing to stop it.

In the Sixties the number of registered heroin addicts mushroomed – from only sixty-eight in 1959 to 2240 in 1968 – and for the first time heroin eclipsed morphine as the main drug of addiction. The first newspaper headlines of 'heroin epidemic' appeared and shocked the public with tales of 'junkies' and 'dropouts' hanging round the West End of London where a black market in drugs of all sorts was flourishing.

At the beginning of the decade, heroin addicts tended to be middle-class, often middle-aged, lonely and isolated individuals. They came from all over the country but tended to gravitate to certain haunts in London's West End: North Oxford Street pubs, Boots at Piccadilly Circus and 'junkies' corner' – the junction of Haymarket and Coventry Street. Their life could be chaotic – sleeping rough, chasing 'junkie doctors' round Soho in search of a 'fix'. Dr John Petro used to prescribe heroin at £3 a shot in the buffet at Baker Street Underground station and a variety of West London hotels.

The Brain Committee was reconvened in 1964 and this time acted more decisively to stem the growth of the black market and the spread of addiction. Lord Brain told the Home Office, 'Your problem can be summed up in two words – Doctor X.' Brain II left the power with the medical profession – but concentrated in the hands of a select few doctors. Heroin and cocaine could now be handed out only by doctors at special new drug clinics.

The second half of the 1960s was a time when thousands of teenagers were experimenting with new drugs – cannabis, amphetamines and the psychedelic drug LSD. Kenneth Leech, a priest working in Soho, wrote vivid accounts of Carnaby Street where beads, bells and Indian clothes were sold to 'flower children' who urged 'make love, not war' and smoked pot, and Soho coffee-bars and discothèques which were filled with 'pill-popping' young-sters at the weekend.

At first this world was quite separate from the heroin set. But the bridge came with the methedrine craze which hit Soho. Young drug users graduated from their pills to this injectable amphetamine which introduced them to 'needle culture'. From here to heroin was a small step. The number of known heroin addicts more than quadrupled from over 500 in 1965 to 2240 in 1968 – and over 300 of them were under 20.

Despite the reports of a 'heroin epidemic' heroin use in the Sixties was not comparable to our present problem. It did not become part of Sixties' youth culture. Kenneth Leech, said that it tended to be the most disturbed and confused young people who took to heroin. At least two studies carried out at the time confirmed this was true.

The first appearance of an imported black market was in September 1967 when police found a light-brown granular substance which turned out to be a mixture of heroin and caffeine, part of a consignment from Hong Kong. It cost £60–80 per ounce wholesale, and was intended for smoking by the Chinese community in London. But a group of British addicts were injecting themselves with it too. They had made contact with Chinese pushers of the 'brown sugar' in a billiard hall in Soho, probably by chance.

At first, main-liners who were used to pharmaceutical heroin of high purity and strength were suspicious of this impure mixture. But, at £1.50 a grain (60mg), it was cheaper than pharmaceutical heroin, and it soon became an established 'fix'. In 1969, just over sixty samples of illicit heroin were found by police, compared to two the year before. There were drawbacks to using Chinese heroin – it carried a high risk of accidental overdose or infection because its strength and purity varied greatly. But it continued to circulate on the streets of London's West End until the mid-Seventies when patterns of international trafficking changed. The advent of Chinese heroin also made the heroin scene more businesslike as there were many 'professional' non-addicted dealers peddling it.

There is a widely held view that from 1965 to the late Seventies, the British heroin problem was held in check. The only indicator available – the number of new addicts registered with the Home Office – suggests that this is not true. Although the number of heroin addicts appeared to drop after 1968, there was a steady increase in the number of 'opiate addicts'. This was because heroin addicts were put on to heroin substitutes by drug clinics from 1968 onwards. Many of them continued to use illegal heroin, but this was not 'registered'.

But from 1977 the heroin addiction figures began to escalate and in July 1979 newspapers carried grim warnings of a coming 'heroin epidemic'. The Standing Conference on Drug Abuse (the watch-dog body for drug agencies in the voluntary sector) declared that the British clinic-treatment system had failed to control the spread of addiction. By 1983 there were 4786 registered heroin addicts, probably only a small fraction of the true number. This was mainly because of a new source of seemingly limitless amounts of black market heroin – South-West Asia.

One of the first European countries to feel the effects of the wave of cheap, mass-produced South-West Asian heroin was Germany – and by the end of 1979 the news magazines there were full of stories about the new plague of heroin addicts. The large numbers of Turkish migrant workers that were employed there provided a perfect cover for the traffickers, and heroin soon started streaming into the rest of Europe. The Turks successfully challenged the Oriental hold of the European market in what had been its strong-hold of Amsterdam, and were able to provide regular deliveries of heroin from South-West Asia – unlike the Chinese groups' erratic and dwindling supply of heroin from the Golden Triangle.

Also muscling in on the burgeoning market were Lebanese, Syrian and Pakistani traffickers, as well as some enterprising Europeans – all smuggling heroin which had been converted from South-West Asian opium. It was cheaper than the Oriental brands, more potent, and in abundant supply – a market winner. Like Germany and the Netherlands, Italy quickly capitulated, becoming a key transit country for heroin on its way from the Golden Crescent to the rest of Europe, and also a location for heroin laboratories which supplied the drug to America.

Britain had its first taste of cheap heroin when the fall of the Shah of Iran sent Iranian refugees into this country in 1979 – some of whom brought their wealth with them in the form of the convenient commodity of heroin. Like the rest of Europe, South-West Asian heroin began to seep into Britain, filling up the gap left when the Iranians' heroin had been gobbled up. By 1982, heroin from the Golden Crescent accounted for 82 per cent of British customs seizures of the drug. Roy Penrose, the head of the Metropolitan police drugs squad, describes it as a 'hurricane of heroin' which 'commands a share of the market that many multinational companies would be very proud of'.

Although the traditional overland routes first used by cannabis smugglers have been followed, this country was an ideal direct destination for heroin from South-West Asia, given the strong cultural, commercial and trading links with Pakistan and the Indian sub-continent. In June 1984, customs officers at Felixstowe found their largest haul of heroin ever – 40 kilos in a shipment of brass ornaments from Karachi. The drug, which had a street value of about £6 million, had been neatly hidden in tubes inserted in the hollowed-out planks of five wooden packing cases, which were part of the cargo of the German ship *Tristan*.

Heroin is smuggled into this country in a variety of bizarre and imaginative ways. Couriers swallow condoms full of the drug, or hide it in their body cavities – 'the stuffers and the swallowers' as they are known to customs men. The unlucky ones, like a Nigerian woman who swallowed twenty-seven packets of heroin sealed in polythene and Sellotape, die of massive overdoses when the drug leaks out into their stomachs.

Another favourite method is to hide the heroin in false compartments in briefcases and suitcases. Heroin has also been found in beautifully crafted chess sets; packed into walnuts and bread rolls; in bottles of brandy; and even hidden in a consignment of tombstones.

But it is much simpler to use bribery. Bribery has become a way of life for many established smugglers in Pakistan, whose regular costs include bribes for police, customs, airport security and bureaucrats – before the heroin has even left the country for Europe. Heroin is openly on sale in the three great smugglers' bazaars in the tribal lands of the north-west frontier – Bara, Landi Kotal and Darra. And there are reports from Karachi that the police cast a blind eye to heroin dealing in the market on the outskirts of the city. Perhaps even more worrying, the 200,000 to 500,000 addicts that are part of the rapidly spreading problem in Pakistan are said to include people in the police, customs and airport security.

Bribery does not stop in Pakistan, but is used to smooth the way in this country, by paying staff at airports and harbours to pick up the heroin before it goes through customs, and take it in via a back route. At the end of 1983, one such smuggling operation was discovered, importing millions of pounds worth of heroin via a cleaning company at Heathrow. The staff of the company worked in all parts of the airport, including the lounges and arrival areas which passengers passed through before customs control. The staff supervisor, a 43-year-old man named Sarup Singh Balu, had been approached by a Pakistani trafficking group to help get heroin into Britain. His brother, Inderjeet Singh Balu, who worked with him, collected a holdall containing over 17 kilos of heroin in October 1983 from an Indian courier travelling on a British Airways flight from Delhi. Balu left with the holdall via an emergency exit – and was arrested before he could deliver the heroin in his cleaning van.

There is no single most-favoured method of heroin smuggling, but instead continuous changes and variations to thwart customs.

By 1983, Drug Enforcement Administration intelligence was pointing to Sri Lankans joining the swelling army of couriers. They were buying heroin in Pakistan and India, frequently concealing it in the soles of their shoes, or in toothpaste tubes, or inside their bodies. Apart from those old favourites, they hid heroin under overcoat collars, inside leg seams, and in the bottom hems of trousers. Nigerian couriers were also stepping in as pack-horses for the wave of South-West Asian heroin, with Lagos emerging as the main African trans-shipment point for heroin on its way to Western Europe and America.

At the same time, Spain was increasing in importance, as the site of negotiations for major trafficking organizations – and as a convenient place for couriers to get off their flights from Pakistan, and hand over their packages in transit-lounges to British couriers travelling home on package-holiday flights. According to a customs officer at Heathrow: 'They will go away on a cheap holiday, pick up a consignment of heroin, and then arrive back at Heathrow where they merge in with the crowds of mums and dads, with their buckets and spades and souvenirs from Malaga.' Spain also has the advantage to trafficking organizations of an increasing number of Syrians, Lebanese and Iranians living there, providing a pool of potential couriers on the Middle Eastern routes out of South-West Asia.

Added to this potent mix is the presence of British criminals in Spain, fugitives there from the law, who see the tempting possibility of a painless and profitable investment in drugs. Derek Olley, of the Central Drugs Intelligence Unit, describes it as 'a haven for villainy – what nicer than to sit in the sun and direct operations from over there?' The more enterprising can double their profits with counterfeit currency: 'If you buy $100,000 of forged dollar bills for £25,000, and then pay for the drugs with the forged money, there are two profits to be made. We're beginning to find these deals turning up – indicating that villainy is villainy.'

With so many different nationalities popping up as couriers, financiers and manufacturers, it is not surprising that the trafficking groups are often multinational teams. In 1983, the police stumbled over an extraordinary group of people who had become entwined with each other through the heroin trade – and who are a good example of how distribution works both from Pakistan and inside this country.

The story started when a Pakistani man living in south London, named Mohammed Siddique, visited Pakistan in the autumn of 1982. While he was in Lahore, Siddique was recruited by a trafficking organization, when a man named Choudry approached him to bring heroin back with him into London. Siddique refused this offer, but he did agree to pick up the drugs once they had been smuggled into England.

So in December 1982, when he was back home in Tooting, Siddique rang Choudry in Lahore, who gave him the contact number of the courier he was to meet. Siddique rang the number, and, according to Choudry's instructions, asked for 'four films'. The man who answered the phone agreed to meet him on 17 December, at Platform Seven of London Bridge station – but when Siddique got there, he lost his nerve and ran away before approaching the courier. A hurried international telephone conversation followed, between Siddique and an angry Choudry – who ordered him to make another arrangement to pick up the heroin from the courier. Siddique plucked up his courage and did as he was told. The new meeting place was to be East Grinstead station in Sussex, that same evening. And his contact there was the same man that had come to London Bridge station – a Japanese doctor, wearing a boy-scout uniform, carrying a bag full of heroin.

Siddique, unperturbed by the unusual garb of the courier, collected four kilos of heroin, and returned to Tooting. He dutifully phoned Choudry the next day, having stored the heroin in his chimney, and was told his next task was to go to meet a Cypriot, Panayis Kiriacou, outside Bayswater tube station. They went to a nearby Wimpy bar, and Siddique found out that his payment would be £15,000 – the first instalment of which he would get when he delivered part of the heroin to a basement flat just off Queensway, in Bayswater. Siddique trailed back to Tooting, and came to Bayswater the next morning with about ten ounces of heroin – and was then sent home again by Kiriacou to pick up another 15 ounces. He was paid £9000 by the Cypriot in £10 and £20 notes, and another £2000 over the next few days as he transported two kilos of heroin to the Bayswater flat.

The flat was not Kiriacou's – he owned a house in Ilford – but was rented by a 30-year-old woman called Ruska Shvili. She was a Polish prostitute who had adopted Australian nationality, and was a heroin addict. Kiriacou used her flat to distribute heroin from, and had built up a profitable business there. But he never got the next instalment of heroin to carry on trading. On 1 February 1983, the police raided Siddique's house, where a diligent sniffer dog called Sweep found 2 kilos of heroin hidden up the chimney. A few days later, both Kiriacou and Shvili were arrested.

The police then tried to find out a bit more about the mysterious Japanese gentleman who had materialized at East Grinstead station. They traced his telephone number to a respectable detached house in East Grinstead, where a family of boy-scout enthusiasts lived. They confirmed that they had indeed met a Japanese scoutmaster – a Dr Hisa Yoshi N. Maruymah, whom they called 'Doc'. The family had made friends with Doc in March 1982, at a convention at the headquarters of the Scouting movement in Epping Forest. They had swopped some boy-scout badges, and he told them that he travelled the world for the movement, and was secretary to the High Commissioner for Scouting in Karachi. By the summer they were all firm friends, and Doc came to stay in East Grinstead about once a month, using it as an English base for his worldwide travels. He was a perfect guest, who never touched drink or cigarettes – 'a proper gentleman, very friendly, open and generous', said the family.

The doctor was also a leading heroin courier. In December 1982, he had brought 30 kilos of heroin into Heathrow, from Karachi, in a scout's haversack – of which 4 kilos had gone to Siddique, some to Shvili's flat, some to a Dane in Harwich, some to an Englishman in London, and the rest to a Dutchman. As well as delivering the heroin – which he later claimed he thought was hashish – he also picked up over $1.5 million in payment, to take back to the Pakistan trafficking organization.

He had not yet been paid his £30,000 fee as a trusted courier, when he was arrested at Schiphol airport in Amsterdam in May 1983. The doctor was stopped by customs after he got off a flight from Singapore, via Karachi, carrying a flight-bag containing 17 kilos of heroin. He needed the money, he said, for a clinic in Pakistan. The customs men in Holland were unimpressed, and Dr Maruymah was sent to prison for ten years. As far as the police in London know, the Pakistani organization that employed him continues to work unabated.

Despite the increasing importance of South-West Asian heroin since 1979, it does not have a total stranglehold on the market. About 7 per cent of seizures are now coming from the production areas of the Middle East – from places like the Bekaa Valley, where the heroin industry is gaining hold because of the unsettled situation in Lebanon. Like the frontier of Pakistan and Afghanistan, opium is becoming an important commodity to pay for guns and to finance wars.

And heroin is also beginning to flow again from the Golden Triangle of Burma, Laos and Thailand, providing about 11 per cent of UK seizures. 'No sooner than one stamps on one area, another emerges,' said David Mellor in August 1984, with a trace of weariness. 'We are more often in the business of containment.' After the poor crops of the late 1970s, the harvest is flourishing again, with about 650 tonnes of opium gathered in the 1982–3 crops. According to Drug Enforcement Administration intelligence, the rebel forces of the Burmese Communist Party dominate opium-poppy cultivation, and the Shan United Army controls heroin production in the jungle no-man's land along the Thai-Burmese border. Although government military operations had some success in disrupting the flow of chemicals needed for heroin manufacture, more than a dozen laboratories were still operating along the border in 1983.

A large amount of the opium crop is either used by the hill-tribe poppy growers, or used in other parts of South-East Asia – but the rest is smuggled out via Bangkok, Tokyo, Seoul, Singapore or Hong

Kong. DEA intelligence believed that in 1983, a South-East Asian heroin trafficking organization successfully smuggled about 60 kilos of heroin into New York, via London and Toronto.

There are some British customs officers who say privately that England is not only a convenient staging-post for trafficking, it is also a soft touch for the heroin traders because of the ease with which they are able to move drugs in and out of the country. Although the drug investigations division of Customs and Excise has been increased from 121 in 1979, to 212 posts, and sixty new uniformed officers were appointed in 1984, 'the thin blue line' is, as the epithet suggests, heavily overstretched. Overall, Customs and Excise has lost 1000 staff since 1979 – of which about 800 were in front-line customs controls. According to the Customs and Excise Group of the Society of Civil and Public Servants, 'a crisis point has been reached', with only one in 100 passengers at Dover and Heathrow being questioned, and at peak times one in 400.

At peak holiday periods up to 5000 people an hour stream into Heathrow airport – yet the number of customs officers on duty to deal with them is the same as ten years ago despite an 80 per cent increase in the number of passengers. At times of meal-breaks, one officer may be left on his own, to watch over 1000 people passing by. One of the customs officers at the airport says, 'It is very frustrating to be on your own and faced with a whole jumbo-load of passengers. The smugglers are fully aware of what is happening, and know that there is minimal cover.'

The story is the same at Britain's seaports. At the height of the summer, more than 400 cars, fifty coaches and thousands of foot passengers arrive at Dover every hour of the day. 'From June to September, each officer in the green lane has to deal with one car every forty-five seconds,' says Norrie Phillips, a local officer. 'It takes at least an hour to search a car properly, so it doesn't take much to cause a huge backlog. There is a jam whenever there is a drug seizure, or when officers go on meal-break, and then the only way to relieve the pressure is to wave the cars through.'

In the last three years there has been an 86 per cent increase in the number of coaches arriving at Dover, but only four extra staff have joined customs to deal with them. According to a report by the Customs and Excise group of the Society of Civil and Public Servants: 'This has led to nearly automatic clearance of coaches at Dover without proper customs checks.'

The resources of customs staff checking ships have also been stretched, so that in some ports less than 20 per cent of vessels are searched when they arrive in Britain. Before 1977, every single one would have been boarded by Customs officers on arrival – but since then the system of having rummage crews of searchers based in a port has been phased out in favour of having mobile crews who are expected to cover several ports – with fewer officers.

According to a local-branch secretary of the customs officers' union at Felixstowe: 'We're losing the drugs battle, there's no question ... We're a laughing-stock. We know there's smuggling going on but just haven't got the staff to deal with it.' His area of East Anglia used to have crews of specialist ship-searchers based at Felixstowe, King's Lynn, Great Yarmouth and Harwich, plus two mobile crews. There are now only three mobile crews for the whole area – and of 500 ships which came into Felixstowe in the first quarter of 1984, only one was thoroughly searched, or 'rummaged' as it is known in the trade.

David Mellor has dismissed the Society of Civil and Public Servants' arguments of understaffing as simply a union battle for 'more bottoms on seats'. In a heated debate in the Commons in July 1984, he said that adding to the number of customs officers at ports and airports would cause the whole system of controls to grind to a halt: 'We have to be realistic about this. Delays already cause anger and frustration at ports and airports.' He emphasized that the number of investigations officers had increased, and it was their intelligence work that would stop heroin coming into this country: 'Above all, we want good coordinated intelligence, leading to the smashing of conspiracies and to the arrest of the Mr Bigs and not just the small fry, who are two-a-penny because of the level of bribes which are being offered to people to bring the stuff through the airports.'

But heroin does not just come in through airports and big ports, but by sea to isolated coves and beaches. Good intelligence may give an idea of where traffickers plan to land – but it cannot always be specific, and can never point to every smuggling operation. Yet uniformed officers can only provide a limited general patrol. There are only three customs men on night duty for the whole of the east coast of Scotland, and two for the South Wales' coast. Two officers, with one car between them, cover the coastline from Caernarvon to Fleetwood – and Merseyside airport at Speke. There are times when only one covers the entire 500 miles of coastline in Devon and Cornwall.

According to one officer in Plymouth, the customs men are sometimes powerless to stop heroin brought in on private yachts. 'At Heathrow and Dover all the arrivals are channelled through one place, but here people can land anywhere, at any time of the day ... There are hundreds of little creeks and inlets where smugglers can sail four or five miles inland at high tide. Then all they need is access to a quiet road, and they're away.' Regular coast patrols have now been reduced, and Plymouth's sniffer dogs were moved to Bristol. 'All we can do is hope to be in the right place at the right time,' he says.

Smuggling is made easier by the fact that yachts are subject only to voluntary customs control. Skippers are supposed to notify officers of their arrival and departure, but it is impossible to tell how many ignore this control – or how many unload drugs and then report their arrival. Richard Locke, at the Customs and Excise Group of the Society of Civil and Public Servants, estimates that about half of the yachts arriving from abroad do not bother to report at all – 'and even if they did all check in, there just isn't the customs staff to provide even a semblance of control'.

As heroin becomes more and more available, with no sign of the price going up, some customs officers are becoming angry and frustrated. One man in Dover, faced with a busy summer season and no extra customs manpower, said: 'We just have to have more customs men to stop the spread of addiction. I see the junkies in Dover, I know the pubs where they buy it. I don't want to see my own two children going the same way – because no family is safe.

We're at the sharp end in customs, we can see what is going on – and yet we're powerless to stop it.'

It is a bitter historical twist that a century ago in another country, politicians, civil servants and families watched the alarming spiral of drug addiction with the same feeling of helplessness. The country was China in the nineteenth century. The drug-trafficking organization was the British Empire (see Appendix).

But while historians may judge that Britain is receiving its just deserts for a discreditable past, this is little consolation to frustrated parents today whose children are addicted to heroin. After 14 kilos of heroin were seized in Liverpool in April 1984, when a ship carrying a cargo of animal-feed arrived from Pakistan, their frustration threatened to boil over into blind rage. A mother from Merseyside, who had joined a local parents' self-help group after her son became an addict, said: 'Are our children dying to boost Pakistan's ailing economy, or finance Afghanistan's war? ... Believe me, the parents are well aware of Pakistan's involvement in the trade, and are very, very angry. Last week, when a large supply of heroin was found on a Pakistani ship docked at Liverpool, the parents at our meeting wanted to arrange for this ship to be burnt out. The moderates at the meeting – me and a few other mothers – talked them out of it, but believe me this is not idle talk, it will happen.'

[3] Addicts and the network

'It may be a harsh thing to say, but if heroin addiction were an infectious disease which you or I or our respective members of Parliament were liable to contract, you may rest assured that no effort and no expense would be spared to eradicate the sources of the infection, to prevent by all means the entry of infection into this country and to isolate and cure anyone unfortunate enough to have contracted it,' said Lord Lane, the Lord Chief Justice. He was speaking at the annual Judges' Dinner in London in July 1984 and he continued: 'Heroin is not an infectious disease like cholera or typhoid. It is worse ... Heroin is no longer simply a problem of Piccadilly Circus and Leicester Square. It is countrywide from the respectable suburbs of London to Liverpool, Glasgow, Edinburgh and indeed every big city in the country.'

In fact, the judges who assembled to listen to him at the Mansion House may well have been touched by the 'infection', through their families or young friends who had used heroin. A few of their MPs certainly had children or close relations who were addicts. The 'infection' has already spread right across the spectrum of British life – from council estates in London, Liverpool and Glasgow, to Oxford colleges and prestigious public schools. The hundreds of letters and telephone calls we received in response to a series of *Sunday Times* articles about heroin in 1984, were about addicts whose parents were doctors, dentists, nurses, teachers, cooks, barmaids, MPs, businessmen and peers of the realm. As the sister of one young addict said: 'You start by thinking you are the only family with this problem, and then everyone you talk to seems to know someone on heroin.'

Overwhelmingly, the factor that encourages people first to try heroin is its easy availability and cheapness. One Oxford graduate, who first used heroin when she was 19, said: 'I didn't go out looking for it – it suddenly seemed to be everywhere.' That message was echoed throughout the country. A mother from the Wirral, who wrote to the *Sunday Times* after discovering that her 18-year-old son was a heroin addict, said, 'We cannot seem to find a reason for this, only its availability. It is cheaper than cannabis, and at £5 per bag it costs the same as five-and-a-half pints of beer. Apparently the kick is greater.'

Another mother, from Southport, wrote about her 20-year-old son who was using heroin, and said: 'The drugs problem is very widespread in Merseyside, in fact, according to a local police officer, it is the blackest spot in the country. Drugs of any kind are very easily obtainable in pubs and clubs, so easily it makes one wonder if big business is involved.' Estimates vary about the number of people using heroin in Merseyside – but there may be over 2000 addicts. Merseyside Drugs Council has seen a rapid escalation of young people asking them for help. In 1984, 500 heroin users went to the council's centre – almost double the 288 who came in 1983. In 1984, they treated forty-five young children under the age of 16 who were using heroin, and another ninety-two in the 16 to 18 age group. Drugs-council staff believe that this represents only a fraction of the problem. They guess that 30 per cent of young people in Merseyside use heroin. The official Home Office figures for the country as a whole show that the number of addicts notified annually more than trebled, from 3023 in 1973 to 10,235 in 1983. These figures represent only the tip of an iceberg, because some doctors do not register the addicts they are treating with the Home Office, and many addicts do not have treatment – and so slip through the net. The Home Office admits that the real number of addicts may be as high as 50,000.

What their figures do show is that addicts are becoming younger; between 1980 and 1983 the proportion of new addicts notified to the Home Office who were aged under 21 increased from 16 to 21 per cent (from 257 in 1980 to 879 in 1983). Overall, the trend revealed by the Home Office figures is alarming: in 1982 there were 2793 new addicts registered with the Home Office; in 1983 the number was 4200 – an increase of more than 50 per cent.

Very little detailed local research had been done, but the Drug Indicators Project, which did a close study of drug use in the London boroughs of Camden and Islington, found that there were about 2000 heroin addicts in the area in 1983, and 2500 in 1984. The project estimated that there were at least as many occasional users of heroin, and probably more. In a report at the end of 1983, the project observed that heroin use was becoming more widespread throughout the country: 'The last two to three years have seen an increasing involvement of much younger people ... Increased availability and use has been particularly noticeable outside London, especially in large urban conurbations such as Manchester, Edinburgh and Glasgow. It has also continued to increase in London.'

The report pointed out that heroin use was increasing in all classes of society: 'In the more depressed parts of some cities, heroin use appears to be developing into a pattern usually associated with the ghetto conditions in some North American cities ... As well as increasing in some working-class communities, heroin has expanded throughout a wide range of social groupings, including the children of the middle and upper classes.'

The response to the *Sunday Times*' articles showed that heroin use was not confined to large cities, but had moved to rural areas. One woman, who lived in a small Devon village, described how her husband had recently started using heroin: 'We had grown up (or thought we had) during the Sixties, when dope-smoking was pretty widely acceptable, and still is amongst many of our age group. At that time heroin was taboo, and junkies looked upon as social pariahs.' Yet after being unemployed for several years, her husband had made the previously forbidden progression to heroin use, and was eventually arrested: 'My daughter is very censorious and disapproving, but I'm sure she'll come round in time, and accept this as a weakness, a human frailty, accelerated probably by the adverse circumstances of continual unemployment. My son however is too young to understand. When my husband is sent to prison, as it surely seems he must be – what then? How do we, the innocent victims, survive the poverty, loneliness, hardship and, perhaps worse, the finger-pointing that is bound to ensue?'

Her story was echoed by many others whose lives were shaken by the appearance of heroin. One doctor who ran a small country practice in Norfolk was 'horrified' to discover that he had three heroin addicts who needed help in the tiny villages that he covered.

One girl, who had started using heroin when she was 18, wrote to say: 'There is nothing new about teenage drug use, it is just there is more of it about, and larger numbers of people are using heroin straight off. Whilst it was a minority occupation it could be safely ignored.' But the problem can no longer be ignored. The new heroin addicts emerging in 1983–4 were not the rootless, social misfits of the Sixties and Seventies. Heroin use was no longer a fringe activity, but was being absorbed into respectable society. A 36-year-old man, who had himself been an addict in the 1960s and given it up in 1976, saw today's heroin use as very different from 'the old days' of the 'small, English gentlemanly hard-drug society'. Nowadays, it was threatening to spread to ordinary children: 'Policemen will have to worry about their children, I'm worried about mine – and what will be the order of the day in the school playground of tomorrow?'

His fears were reflected in the reports which started circulating about 'playground pushers' ensnaring young children on to heroin. In May 1984 there was even a claim made at the Royal College of Nursing conference that food and drink at a school in Birkenhead had been laced with heroin – an allegation that police could find no evidence to back up. There were also rumours up and down the country that young people were being deliberately trapped by Machiavellian dealers. An ex-user of heroin in Glasgow claimed: 'Most of the kids get started on dope and then the dealers give them heroin for nothing. When they've been using it for a while, the dealers start charging them, and by that time the kids really need it.'

But what seems more commonplace is that heroin use spreads amongst groups of friends, a few of whom may be forced into selling it to pay for their own habits. As the mother of a heroin addict wrote, from the small Hampshire village where she lived: 'In my experience, there is no difference between the addict and the pusher.

Every addict has been introduced to the drug by a pusher but, having acquired the habit, every addict will become a pusher in turn (and do anything else) in order to acquire money.'

And although there are major traffickers in Britain, Derek Olley, of the Central Drugs Intelligence Unit at Scotland Yard, says: 'I don't believe there's someone in London sitting behind a big map of the country saying, OK, let's permeate Devon with heroin today. It's more complicated than that. It's like the spread of fashion – there are punk rockers everywhere, skinheads everywhere, in London, Birmingham, small villages and towns up and down the country. Heroin spreads in the same way. Take, just for an example, teenagers in Torquay. They think it's terribly boring in Torquay, and they're a bit cheesed off with cannabis. So they happen to be steaming up to London, and they pick up some heroin, and take it home to Torquay. Before long it's the beginning of a little network. They sell it to their friends, and then a major dealer in the area can step in and provide it wholesale closer to home. Soon there are clearly developed networks, and it's sold at very cheap prices which also help to guarantee a future market.'

By the beginning of 1984, taboos about the drug were broken down, not only because it was so widely available, but also because a new way of using heroin had come into fashion, often accompanied by the myth that heroin consumed in this way was not addictive. 'Chasing the dragon' meant that users did not have to overcome a reluctance to inject themselves. 'Chasing' involves laying a line of heroin on a strip of aluminium foil and heating it from underneath with a lighted match. The powder turns into a bead of black liquid which runs down the foil, giving off pungent fumes that are inhaled through a tube. The craze caught on fast – a young addict from Southwark summed up the feelings of most of his friends in the spring of 1984 when he said, 'When my mate first offered me some, I said there was no way I was going to inject needle. But when he showed me how to chase, it didn't really seem like taking heroin at all.'

The new name for heroin – 'skag' – also removed some of its taboo. Many teenagers in the first wave of users in the sprawling council estates of South London did not even know that their cheap new drug was heroin.

One boy, from what he describes as 'a vast concrete mess sandwiched in the heart of working-class south-east London', described what happened to his friend Jimmy in 1984: 'Jimmy is typical of many of our generation, he quit school early without any exams, but he wasn't thick. He went through various dead-end jobs in sweatshops to supplement the dole. Horrible jobs ... He didn't like it, the wages were low and conditions bad.

'His brother had introduced him to hash early on, but as Jimmy got more cash he experimented. He did speed, coke, nitrate, acid, but not heroin. Heroin was what rich and trendy New Yorkers injected into their arms, it's what you saw on TV. The change happened quickly. The first time Jimmy tried it ["Chasing the dragon"] he felt sick, he puked all over the place. But he didn't know it was heroin. That initial sickness didn't put him off. By the time he found out it was heroin, he was a regular user. He was assured by his mates that if he didn't inject he would be safe. In less than a year he was the complete junky ... The last time I saw him he frightened me, he looked dangerous. It was said he'd gone on the needle, which, if true, could mean that others will also switch to injections rather than sniffing heroin. My aunt lives next door to him, and when he has screaming fits, she forces her 10-year-old son to watch, to scare him away from the white death ...'

Heroin addiction on the council estates of south London was widely publicized throughout 1984, with dramatic newspaper reports about the 'skaggies' or 'skagheads'. It is impossible to tell how many of the local teenagers were using heroin, but there were abundant signs of an epidemic: empty aluminium foil boxes, scorched foil, and burnt matches littered the stairways of the tower blocks, often covered with the bile of those made sick by 'chasing'. On the estates of north Southwark alone, on either side of the Old Kent Road, there were an estimated 1000 young people who had used heroin.

One mother living in one of the council blocks off the Old Kent Road, discovered that her son Darren was using heroin at the end of 1982, when he was 15. All his friends were taking it with him, and by the beginning of 1984 he was in an appalling state: 'He threatened to kill me – or kill himself in front of me. He would run a knife down his arm to make it bleed. I couldn't talk to him anymore. He wasn't interested in anything except getting skag. I'd put my arms round him and cuddle him, but nothing would help.

'When I first found out, nobody knew anything. I told other parents, whose children were on it, but they couldn't believe it about their own children. They just thought it was puff (cannabis). I think the kids don't know what it is to begin with. Darren didn't realize it was heroin when he first started taking it.

'I don't know what the answer is to this problem. It's just too big, just too big. In the streets round here you see hordes of kids looking like zombies. My Mum says there'll be no more kids left in a few years.'

Although the newspaper reports in 1984 tended to focus on the working-class communities of London and Liverpool, heroin addiction was also rocking the middle and upper classes. Heroin is just as cheap and widely available in Knightsbridge and Chelsea as it is in the council estates of Southwark – and for those young people who had already been able to afford cocaine, it was an easy step to sniff another white powder. The first wave of addicts had in turn become pushers, using their own social networks. Hetty started using heroin when she was 17, after leaving public school, buying it from a City insurance broker who sold it to pay for his own habit: 'Soon I ran out of money, so I started dealing for a while – but I usually needed the whole supply for myself, so that didn't work. I didn't pay my rent or the phone bill. Nothing stopped me buying smack. I wasn't interested in paying bills. I started stealing from my parents and then I started stealing cheque books to survive.'

For some middle-class addicts, heroin was an exclusive new fashion. Tom, an ex-public-school boy who used it with most of his friends, explained: 'I suppose I found it rather exciting because of the very taboo nature of it. When walking down the street while on it I felt like laughing at all the people in the street, "Ha ha, suckers! I feel good, bet you don't!"'

Rebecca, also with a public-school education, started taking heroin in 1982, when a friend offered it to her: 'I was just 18, and a lot of my friends had started taking it at the same time ... it was really good fun, and seemed like a good thing to do in your spare time. Once you've started taking smack with your friends, it seems like there's nothing else to do in the evening.'

She carried on taking it at her first year at university, and then gave it up during the summer. But at the beginning of her second year, when she was back in London, she started again. Within a couple of months, she had graduated from sniffing it to injecting it: 'All my schoolfriends were shooting up, and I started taking more and more. I still said that I could give it up, but I couldn't ... I started involving the people I knew who had been shooting up – I injected it for them. I feel so guilty about that now, but at the time you don't care one bit about anybody. It's such a selfish drug.' By the end of her second year at university, Rebecca's parents knew that she was taking heroin, and took her abroad: 'I lay in bed and my mother nursed me. She wouldn't let me out of her sight. But after a few days I forced her to let me go out, and I'd go and score – you can find smack anywhere in Europe. I jacked up [injected] in my feet, so that my parents wouldn't see the track marks.'

Rebecca, who is now a model, finds it hard to explain why someone with such a privileged, golden life, should need the cocooning effects of heroin: 'I don't know why – except me and my friends have all had too much, too early, too easily. I didn't have anything to work for. It's all been too easy. I can always do what I want to do.'

Sarah, who was at the same exclusive public school, and then started using heroin when she went to Oxford, agrees that it was not to escape from a grey world without prospects, but an exciting, glamorous drug taken by a social élite: 'It was our new toy for the first few months – we were a bunch of hedonists out for the biggest kicks. I suppose we knew it was dangerous – but we had a certain arrogance. We thought that we were intelligent and could control the drug. We couldn't imagine becoming depraved junkies. In fact we thought we were the ultimate in cool.'

Within a year she had started injecting it, and her addiction continued through her second year at university: 'It made my social group even more élitist – we adopted a devil-may-care attitude and no one ever rejected us. I was invited to lots of parties, and none of my tutors ever said anything, even though I'd turn up stoned to a tutorial ... Oxford seemed to be the perfect place to be a junkie.' By then she was spending all of her student grant, and running up a huge overdraft to support her habit.

It was not until the end of her second year at university that Sarah began to worry: 'I had never really tried to give it up properly till then. I started to hate myself and the life I was living, so I tried to stop, but I couldn't. I'd sunk into total depths.' Desperate for money, she went to London to try and find a job: 'If I didn't work, I couldn't score, but if I didn't have any junk, I couldn't work.'

She managed to pull through that crisis, and kept her habit under control when she went back to Oxford. But two years after heroin had been introduced as a fun new drug, many of her friends were still heavily addicted: 'It has this incredible power over people, whatever their class or background. It's difficult to cut yourself off from friends, but I take junk when it's offered, so I know I've just got to steer clear of it. That is increasingly hard.'

But it is not enough to point to increased availability and the dissolving of taboos as the only reasons for the widespread use of heroin. Amanda, a young heroin addict, who wrote a long letter to the *Sunday Times*, pointed out that not everyone chooses to use heroin: 'It is the quality of life or the lack of it which determines who will become an addict and who will not. Some people will prefer to live in a fantasy world, whatever the cost in real terms, rather than face the reality of a world in which they feel powerless ... The identity of the junkie, however ludicrous it may appear to whoever reads this, is better than none at all.'

She said that whatever else she did in her life, heroin was always more appealing: 'I will always be a junkie in my mind. No matter how much I keep myself occupied, whatever new diversions I create, when it comes down to the nitty-gritty, irrespective of what I do, it turns out to be another smack substitute. I have never found

45

anything else to replace the intensity, the power or the inner peace and silence which it gives.'

She gave a graphic account of the effect of the drug: 'I follow the coldness of the smack up my arm, five seconds and it will hit me, a five-quid jolt. White lightning, like electricity, the headrush is a powerful thing – it cannot be described, only experienced. I feel warm, at peace, nothing can touch me, drifting, flowing on a dreamlike quality. Must remember to remove the needle, not much cop if I doze off like this, dribbling blood through the night. Is this really what I am coming to? I just don't care. I can rationalize to eternity and back, whoever is making vast profits out of this situation, what it does for me and others, I know all this, it maims, it scars, it kills – I can read death and destruction in any newspaper. It has no impact. The big events of the world are external to me . . . I dream . . . apathy rules the day.'

An ex-addict in Woking put it more simply: 'While I was under the influence, it was another world, a world of make-believe, you could look at a fairy story book and the pictures seemed to come alive.'

The comment that addicts make over and over again about using heroin is that it offers them immense warmth and comfort. 'You feel totally comfortable in whatever position you are in, no aches or pains anywhere,' wrote Tom in his diary. 'The trouble with coming off is that suddenly you have to face the real world with all its pain, heartache, and coldness, which after being secluded for a while seems almost unbearable; like coming out of a really comfortable hotel room where everything is done for you, and being kicked into the street to find your own way about.

'It is a vicious circle because the more you take, the less you care about, and with nothing to care about, the more you take.'

All of this leads to addicts withdrawing further and further into their own cocoons. Maureen, who was a heroin addict for sixteen years before she gave up, is very clear about the dramatic contrast between the pleasure she got from the drug, and the appalling effects it had on her life: 'The effect of heroin, which I always injected, seemed to me to be a warm comforting buzz. All those nasty painful emotions were stifled. No need for love: sex came a very poor second or third, and then disappeared altogether as a need.

'On the other hand, every time I experienced withdrawal symptoms – which was once a day at least – my emotions ran the gamut from weeping to laughing to furious anger. My nerves did merry dances on their own. I had stomach cramps and vomited green bile.'

She describes the ancient coat she wore during her years of addiction: 'Eighteen cigarette burns on the front and, inside the sleeves, dark stiff areas of dried blood from the elbows down ... It was filthy, decrepit, verminous looking, and I really didn't care. That is the thing I remember most about being an addict – the fine disregard for the niceties of life that it induces.

'Despite all my repulsive attributes I had friends, nice people, not driven entirely by pity, who would support me and even explain me to their kids – though how, I'll never know. They would take me home, feed me, clean me, give me fresh sheets. I usually responded with love and thievery.'

The stealing that many addicts are forced into adds to their problems – and to the problems of those around them – forcing them even further into their own unreal world. One boy, writing about the effect of heroin addiction on his best friend, described how both the family and surrounding community of Southwark were undermined by heroin: 'His mother, like all mothers, is at her wits' end. She's tried everything. She gave him money, but that made him worse. She tried to chuck him out, but couldn't; she cut off his cash, so he swapped the TV for skag ... He offered me a video recorder for £70, but I turned him down – I couldn't buy it because I knew it was stolen from poor people on the estate, and secondly because I knew all the £70 would go on skag ... Our estates are plagued by break-ins and muggings to get skag cash. No one is immune.'

A mother in Southwark described how she got caught up in the nightmarish world of her 15-year-old son's addiction: 'I tried to help him with money, to keep him from stealing things, so I started giving it to him, £5 in the morning, and another £5 in the afternoon.' But that wasn't enough, and he started stealing from shops, and from her: 'He had been pawning my jewellery, and giving me the ticket so I could get it back. Then he'd steal the pawn ticket, and get some more money, till I couldn't afford to get my jewellery back. Or he'd take money from me. He said he couldn't help it if a fiver was there – it was so easy.'

By the beginning of 1984, when he was 16, he had run away: 'He was living on the roof of this block of flats, in a little place where the water-tank is. He had no friends left – he'd robbed all his friends. There were too many people after him. His girlfriend's parents had told her not to see him anymore. He used to beat her up if she didn't hand over money, or jewellery.

'There were a few other kids like him on the roof. Everytime he came down into our flat, he'd steal something. He smashed the windows to get in – he stole all my clothes, clocks, lamps, a coffee percolator – everything he could pick up and walk away with. I Chubb-locked the front door so that he couldn't get the washing machine out and the furniture.'

Some parents who wrote to the *Sunday Times* said that their children's addiction only became apparent to them when household belongings started to disappear: 'Money was being stolen and my sole decent bits of jewellery had gone,' wrote a mother from Merseyside. 'It was only then that I realized something was very wrong. Now, I have to sleep with my purse under my pillow.'

A London primary-school teacher, who discovered her 19-year-old daughter was a heroin addict, explained that the lifestyle an addict is forced into is as horrifying as the fact they are using heroin: 'Most addicts have three sources of acquiring the cash they need to feed their habit; pushing drugs to other people, stealing and prostitution. Somehow you have to live with the knowledge that your child is probably indulging in one – perhaps all three – methods, and with the inevitable guilt that in some way it must be your fault.' She said that the effect of that guilt is shattering: 'I can't begin to describe the feelings one has in such a situation. I always thought I could cope with anything – if my daughter got pregnant or got VD, or my son got a girl pregnant – anything but drugs.'

That horror is partly the fear of the unknown. Drug education in schools is sporadic, and many parents, teachers and youth workers have only the haziest knowledge about heroin. Such ignorance not only prevents advice being offered to young users – it also adds to the alluring, mysterious quality of heroin, encouraging people to try it.

In June 1984, a report by the Advisory Council on the Misuse of Drugs criticized the inadequacy of preventive measures, and called for continuous training for teachers and youth-workers so that they could educate their pupils about drugs, and cope with any problems that might arise in schools.

But the council emphasized that this should be part of general health education for children. It warned against such ideas as a national advertising campaign that might further glamorize drugs, and encourage young people to experiment.

David Mellor, the Home Office minister at the head of a working-party on drugs, responded with enthusiasm, telling the House of Commons in a debate on drug abuse in July 1984: 'Plainly the constructive use of leisure and giving people meaning and purpose in life is of the essence. Often a rebellion against the life that people lead, and life in the community, leads people into the problem. That is why engaging the sympathies of teachers, parents and those who work with young people, and better coordination, is so important, as the Advisory Council on the Misuse of Drugs stated in its splendid report on prevention ... It makes it clear where the way forward lies.'

But by the beginning of 1985, the government had veered away from the Council's advice, and in February unveiled a £2 million national advertising campaign. The campaign included leaflets for parents and teachers, which were welcomed as being useful. But professionals in the drugs field were dubious about the television campaign aimed at teenagers, although the government emphasized that it was intended to rob heroin of any glamour by emphasizing some of its drearier consequences.

David Turner, of the Standing Conference on Drug Abuse, feared that not only would the television campaign create more, not less interest in heroin, but any good it might do in sending addicts for treatment would be futile: 'The only thing that the advertising might achieve is a demand for services, advice and information which we can't provide. This will lead to more distress and difficulties. The government would have done much better to ensure that services are properly funded and able to meet needs. Then it should have geared its advertising to sending people to treatment and advice services ... as it is, the priorities seem to be very wrong.'

Without proper preventive measures, the spiral of addiction will continue as more addicts have to become pushers in order to support their own habits. And that leaves the police to mop up the problems of addiction – and they may not be able to break the destructive spiral that draws more and more people into heroin use.

[4]   The police response

The heroin addict's first contact with authority is likely to be a police officer. Long before he or she sees a doctor, social worker or voluntary agency who can help fight the habit, the long arm of the law will reach out to punish. One of the major hazards of using heroin is that it is against the law. This in itself can have a disastrous effect on an addict's already chaotic lifestyle – to add to their problems with health, families and work, they also have to cope with police attention and legal proceedings. There are heavy penalties for getting involved with heroin under the Misuse of Drugs Act – up to seven years' imprisonment is possible for the mere possession of heroin.

More severely, heroin use tends to draw addicts into a web of other criminal activities in order to raise the money to pay for an increasingly expensive habit. Burglary, credit-card fraud, stealing cheque books, HP fraud, prostitution and dealing in heroin itself are all common crimes that bring young addicts to the courtroom. Statistics show that the number of drug users coming into conflict with the law has climbed. The number of people found guilty of or cautioned for heroin offences in Britain increased from 435 in 1973 to 1508 in 1983. And many more will have been convicted of burglaries and other crimes as a direct result of drug use. Lothian police estimated in 1984 that over 30 per cent of those arrested for theft and housebreaking in Edinburgh over a six-month period had links with drug abuse.

So heroin addicts tend to regard the police as enemies. The hippy slang of the 1960s, with words like 'pigs' and 'hassles', is still used. The common use of drug-squad officers' first names is a sign of familiarity tinged with contempt. Richard, a 22-year-old ex-addict who was interviewed by *Police Review* last year, said that the police are the 'natural adversary of the junkie'. The police searched him, raided his house and pulled him into the station many times during two-and-a-half years of daily heroin use: 'At first there was not much hassle from the police. The local police knew the regular users, those that had been taking heroin for the last ten to fifteen years. But once the police caught on that there were lots of people taking it regularly, there was lots of hassle, although they didn't catch many.'

Richard's antagonism to the police was tempered with amusement at their ineffectiveness: 'Raids on houses were useless – the gear was always stashed outside. But on one occasion I was at a party that was raided when there was a lot of heroin about. There were about ten people in this room and, because it was a party, we had the dimmer switch turned right down. The police went around with torches and never turned the switch up. Did they think we always lived like that? In the murky darkness everyone managed either to swallow their packs or throw them on the fire.'

Richard says heroin users are bound by a 'code of honour' to protect each other – one person will take the rap for several others, and it's not done to name names during police questioning. Addicts are also very cunning. For these reasons 'the police aren't going to stop it,' says Richard. 'I think it would be helpful if junkies got more sympathetic treatment from the police. They shouldn't be treated on the level of a burglar – they're people with a problem.'

Top policemen all over the country claim that police attitudes to drug addicts have already changed. Chief Constable Barry Price, head of the Cumbria Police Force, says, 'It's interesting to hear people at the operational end now talking of the drug users as victims. They only used to be thought of as offenders. Now, clearly because of the insidious market aimed at young people which they can see them sucked into, officers who work with drug addicts can't help seeing them as victims.'

Peter Imbert, chief constable of Thames Valley police, went even further than this at the annual police drug conference in 1984 with a piece of advice that made many drug help-agencies baulk. He urged parents of drug users to come down to the police station and have a chat about their children's drug problems, assuring them: 'We are not concerned about prosecuting the victim. The victims are offenders, but they are more offended against than offending.'

Detective Superintendent Derek Olley, until July 1985 the deputy head of the Central Drugs Intelligence Unit, which shares the fourth floor of New Scotland Yard with some of Britain's top detectives in the Criminal Intelligence Branch, says that resources are being directed towards catching the dealers instead of the addicts: 'Generally speaking, the chief constables realize that the best deployment is aimed at the dealer rather than the street-level user. So rather than just sending the men out and nicking fifty junkies, the common approach now is to post men at strategic places.'

Users are still being picked up, 'but they're not being grabbed by the collar and pilloried'. They will be asked for information about who is supplying them with heroin and the court will be told that they are users and not dealers. 'It's impossible for a police officer to ignore a heroin user. We get a lot of pressure from parents and teachers to nick them. But there's still a lot of compassion.'

One tangible form of the new compassion is the policy of cautioning first-time drug users that is being followed in some police areas. In 1982, Merseyside police started cautioning people who had cannabis for personal use. Chief Inspector Peter Deary of Merseyside Drug Squad says, 'Cautioning has a very good effect – less than 10 per cent of people we cautioned have come to notice for drug offences again.'

This policy has spread throughout the country, but it is only in London that heroin users are, on occasion, being allowed to go home after a friendly chat about their dealers, with nothing more than a strict word of warning. Detective Chief Superintendent Roy Penrose, head of the Central Drugs Squad in the Metropolitan Police, says, 'If a parent comes in and says "my daughter is using heroin, it's devastating the home", and inquiries show that the young lady hasn't been engaged in crime, then I believe a caution would be the right thing.' The Home Office is keen to get this 'cautioning policy' established elsewhere in the country.

But how accurate is this picture of sympathetic police officers counselling worried parents and troubled addicts throughout the land? Various factors make it difficult for police to live up to the image. One problem is that few heroin addicts remain simply 'victims' who can just be cautioned and sent home. Most of them do turn to stealing or dealing to maintain their habit. And the police do not usually show leniency to these people: more and more of them are landing in court and facing prison sentences.

There is pressure from some quarters for the police to act more harshly and efficiently. Some conservative politicians call for ever more swingeing measures to tackle the heroin menace. Detectives on the ground with years of experience of the drug problem sometimes take a harder line than their superiors.

One tough-minded detective in a provincial police force in England is very much opposed to the new lenient approach: 'They tell us – aim at the pushers, don't bother with the small fry. But you need to arrest the small ones to build up information on the big ones. Senior officers haven't been active in the drug squad – they don't know it's changed in the last five years.' He's also against cautioning for heroin users: 'If someone gets caught with heroin it means they've gone past dope and it's the tip of the iceberg.'

He complains that neither senior police nor ordinary policemen on the beat recognize how much crime is related to drugs: 'A druggie gets more and more professional all the time because he's committing crimes every day. He's always looking over his shoulder. Their system in some ways is more professional than our own. The ordinary bobby is just not equipped to chase up that sort of thing.'

Not enough drug users are being arrested, he believes, and greater cunning and new police powers are needed: 'If a druggie gets caught for shop-lifting, we'll do them for shop-lifting but we won't get his house searched. If we did, we might find a drugs list there or a roach (the cardboard 'filter' of a heroin or cannabis cigarette) in the ashtray. When you're assured that someone is dealing with heroin, there should be telephone taps and a facility to see if something is going through the post.'

Such suggestions are rejected vigorously by voluntary organizations who help and sometimes represent drug addicts. For many of them, current police crackdowns are helping neither society nor drug users. They dismiss police declarations of their new-found liberalism as cosmetic: 'The image which the police has tried to promote quite carefully of not being interested in the small user is not borne out at all,' says Jane Goodser, a lawyer who works with Release, the London agency which gives free legal advice and information to drug addicts when they get into trouble.

'The police are still using powers of stop-and-search to clock up convictions. They do have big operations where people are staked out and dealers raided, but a lot of convictions are for personal amounts. The police are so anxious to make an impact on the public mind that they tend to blow things up. Very insignificant people become "Mr Big of Essex", and the judges seem to accept police evidence about these people unquestioningly.'

How much policemen care, how much they do and what they do about heroin addicts varies enormously throughout the country, depending on the knowledge and commitment of senior officers. Derek Olley says, 'The UK response is fragmented. We have forty-three different drug squads with forty-three different chief officers.' The same is true of the courts.

'In one place you'd be caught with a small amount and the judge would jump a supply charge on you. Elsewhere, another judge would accept that it was a personal amount,' says Jane Goodser, the Release lawyer. She has recently done a survey which shows that big cities are setting a trend for heavier sentencing of user-dealers (people who supply small amounts of heroin to finance their own habit) in court. But in country areas they're taking a slightly more liberal attitude.

Scotland seems to be in a category all of its own for police crackdowns and heavy sentencing. David McLaughlin, a worker for SHADA, an Edinburgh self-help group, says, 'The police used to be very tolerant until you stepped too far out of line. They tended to ignore user-dealers. But in October '84 their attitude changed radically. Possession of anything over a £5 packet was tantamount to possession with intent to supply. The sentences are creeping up to the maximum. Someone got eight years for supplying from his house – he was found with 3 grams. If you deal large amounts, you get what you deserve, but someone using and dealing a little needs help.'

In Glasgow, the main complaint is that the police are not getting to grips with the big dealers. In Possil Park, a run-down area of sprawling housing estates, the heroin trade is controlled by two families who are well-known in the area for their violence and for their other main business – money-lending. Alan Ferry, leader of the local Denmark Street Day Project, which gives advice and counselling to drug users, says the police have lost public confidence because of their inability to crack down on these criminals.

'The police seem very reluctant to get involved in that. They keep saying they can't do anything without evidence. The public have lost patience with the police avoiding the big dealers and going for the small fry.' The new heavy sentencing policy in Scotland is hitting mainly the user-dealers who, Alan Ferry says, 'have been driven into dealing because they've got heavily in debt with the money-lenders, who are – of course – the main heroin traffickers.'

Scottish police insist that, in common with other police forces, they are in fact clamping down on the dealers and showing compassion for the addicts. In Scotland, the Procurator-fiscal, and not the police, decides whether users are charged with simple possession or with intent to supply. The police are 'arresting and detaining people who we find dealing – our job is not to compare which sort of dealer is worst,' says Detective Chief Inspector Angus Morrison, the head of Lothian and Borders Drug Squad.

The policing of drugs has always been a highly sensitive area, fraught with pitfalls. London has had the longest and widest experience of drug problems, but the Home Office and senior police officers admit that until very recently there was no properly functioning drug squad in the Metropolitan Police. One senior officer said, 'Drugs investigation is one of the areas that is sus-ceptible to corruption and because of proved instances of police corruption in the past, senior managers have tended to shy away from dedicating resources for this sort of drug abuse. As a result we've ignored the warning signs over the years of the increasing amounts of heroin.'

The full extent of the corruption and malpractice in the Metropolitan Drug Squad in the late Sixties and early Seventies has never been proved. (The best account of it is provided in *The Fall of Scotland Yard* by Barry Cox, John Shirley and Martin Short, Penguin, 1977.) What is certain is that from 1968 to 1971 the tight-knit group of detectives under Detective Chief Inspector Victor Kelaher – who became known as the 'whispering squad' because of their cloak-and-dagger operations – engaged in some bizarre practices.

Kelaher, one of Scotland Yard's brightest young detectives, had close ties with American drug enforcement agencies and adopted their policy of using informants and undercover work. He and his sergeant, Detective Sergeant Nobby Pilcher, also had a store of unorthodox CID policing methods from their days in the Flying Squad. They had a willing team of detectives such as Detective Constable Nick Pritchard, whose long hair and scruffy appearance allowed him to 'infiltrate' the drugs scene.

Under Kelaher's regime, a network of 'licensed dealers' built up – informants who were free to work their 'patch' with the blessing of the Drug Squad as long as they served up their customers as 'bodies' – easy arrests – for the police. Working undercover, drug-squad detectives often set up and took part in deals, arresting the small fry and rewarding their informants, who were often much bigger dealers than those arrested, with a share of the drugs from the 'bust'. While the victims languished in prison, the informants would be back on the streets selling off their 'police drugs' at remarkably low rates.

That was bad enough – and it seriously worried the Home Office when it got wind of it – but Kelaher himself began to get involved in drug-smuggling circles to an extent that has never been satisfactorily explained.

First he was discovered with a prostitute called Roberts and a man called Rosenblatt, when customs men raided a Holland Park flat in search of smuggled furs and jewellery. Roberts was divorced from Kofi Roberts, a Ghanaian drug trafficker Kelaher had sent to prison some years before. The customs men found an expensive gold watch which Kelaher said he had bought for Mrs Roberts from Hatton Garden – although he couldn't remember the name of the dealer who sold it to him. Customs didn't follow this embarrassing discovery up, but stored it in their files for future use.

The customs came across Kelaher again when they were investigating a drug ring of two Arabs from Beirut, a group of West Indian dealers and a Bahamian night-club owner called Basil Sands who were trying to import heroin from the Middle East. In January 1971, long before the customs got on to the track, Sands told Kelaher that the two Arabs were in London trying to sell two kilos of heroin. Kelaher and two detectives immediately met the drug-smuggling team in a fruitless attempt to find buyers for the heroin.

The Arabs then arranged to send 24 lbs of cannabis to Heathrow in a load of 'oriental goods'. The customs, who were on to the operation by now, seized the drugs at the airport but decided to let the rest of the goods go and observe what happened to them.

Kelaher and Sands had arranged for the drugs to go to the Melba House Hotel in Earl's Court. The customs had Sands' phone tapped and knew about this arrangement, although it is doubtful whether they knew about Kelaher's role at this stage. They had the hotel staked out and delivered the goods themselves. Later that evening, as customs officers watched from the house opposite, a taxi arrived at Melba House where Kelaher was waiting to help the cab-driver get the cases in to the taxi. That night customs arrested Kelaher and two of Sands' accomplices. Kelaher was held for five hours, refused to speak and was finally released.

The case blew the Drug Squad apart when it came to light. Kelaher was not charged but, when Sands and the others came to court, it was as if it were Kelaher who was on trial. Defence counsel claimed that Kelaher was intimately involved with protecting Sands during the smuggling operation. Customs officers said in evidence that they had considered arresting Kelaher as part of the conspiracy and the judge had to direct the jury that Kelaher was not on trial, even if they thought he was in the middle of the smuggling ring. Basil Sands, whose defence was that he was working purely as Kelaher's informant, was sentenced to seven years' imprisonment.

The Lancashire Police were called in to investigate Kelaher and his drug squad, but no action was taken. Soon after, however, Kelaher and five of his detectives were charged with falsifying evidence to clinch the prosecution of a family of drug smugglers. Three of the detectives were convicted of perjury, but Kelaher was acquitted.

The Drug Squad was broken up in June 1971, and in April 1974 Kelaher was given a medical discharge from the police force. In May, Alex Lyon, the Minister of State at the Home Office, gave a hint of the official attitude to the scandal in the House of Commons: '... Kelaher has now resigned from the Metropolitan Police Force on grounds of ill-health. I am allowed by the Commissioner to say that had he not done so serious allegations would have been made against him in disciplinary proceedings.'

Derek Olley says, 'I keep my fingers crossed and hope that that was a historical episode. The practice now in the police service is to keep moving people about – to try and prevent them being exposed to temptation. You rely totally on the integrity of police officers. But I'm not naive enough to think there aren't policemen in this country who aren't greedy – we draw our men from society and society is greedy. Through selection and training, we have to look for the ideal, honest men.'

To this day, the Metropolitan Drug Squad has been kept deliberately small. It consists of only thirty-eight officers – not much larger than the drug squad in Edinburgh – who have to concentrate their efforts on 'top-rank criminals'. But recently, disturbing signs may have begun to emerge – in another branch of the London police.

In March 1985 the name of a Flying Squad detective came up during the court-case of a woman who was found guilty of importing heroin from India. Rebecca, the courier, told the court that she had been met at Harwich by the detective, who arrested her on suspicion of armed robbery and then stole a packet containing over half a kilo of heroin from her. She also believed that the detective could have been involved in setting up the trip to India in the first place – the court heard that the trip had been planned and financed by one of his long-term associates.

Both the judge and the prosecution obviously believed much of what the courier alleged. Judge Lloyd told her: 'A proper sentence for you would be at least four years but this is not an ordinary case. I have taken into account that there are bigger fish than yourself caught in the net.' He sentenced her to twenty months. This case is being investigated by Scotland Yard.

The corruption of the past and the experience of organizations like Release led them and many others to question the general relationship between heroin and the law. Release says that the penal system is not suitable for dealing with addicts because it 'makes no effort to rehabilitate people with drug problems'. They argue that giving addicts cheap and legal prescriptions of heroin substitutes for as long as they want is a better method of social control.

Articles in the *New Statesman*, *New Society* and Channel 4's 'Diverse Reports' have all argued that the addict suffers less from the effects of heroin itself than from involvement with an illegal commodity and from the inevitable attention of the police and the law. The argument for legalizing heroin has even appeared in the pages of *The Times*. Peter Kellner wrote in February 1985: 'The solution to the crisis seems obvious. Legalization would cut consumption, wipe out criminal trafficking and ensure that the heroin consumed would be less harmful than much of what is available on the black market.' He proposed a return to the pre-1969 prescription system when doctors could prescribe heroin at their own discretion.

But Professor Griffith Edwards of the Addiction Research Unit at the Maudsley Hospital was quick to reply in the letters' page: 'The pre-1969 period which Mr Kellner now pictures as a halcyon era was in fact a decade during which heroin addiction disastrously escalated and when exactly the policies he now seeks to resurrect were found to be inadequate ... The policies which were instituted in 1969 for a time did much to bring the epidemic under control.'

There is certainly no clear evidence to suggest that legalization would cut consumption or criminality. The surveys conducted in Glasgow and London during the Seventies to investigate whether or not prescribing heroin or methadone to addicts achieved a lower rate of drug use and criminality among the users were ambiguous. The London survey showed that those prescribed heroin were slightly less 'criminal' than those prescribed methadone, while in Glasgow the methadone users were less 'criminal' than those who had no prescriptions at all.

But the results did not produce a cut-and-dried case for legalization. In Glasgow, the main crime of the group not being prescribed drugs seemed to be using illegal drugs. Prescribing more opiates had no effect on the numbers of local pharmacy thefts, a common drug-related crime. Both clinics stopped prescribing heroin substitutes soon after – the effect on the crime rate was not enough to justify prescribing drugs. And in general, by the mid-Seventies, clinics began to see that prescribing opiates had not prevented a large-scale organized black market from emerging.

As long as the black market continues to exist, few on either side of the argument would disagree that the police should do their utmost to get to the top-level criminals who make vast profits from importation and distribution of heroin in this country. Leon Brittan, the Home Secretary, said in 1983, 'The police know full well that drug trafficking lies at the heart of many criminal conspiracies involving robbery, vice and violence. They know that increasingly the armed robber and gang leaders of yesterday are turning their attention to drug trafficking.' To combat this, two major weapons are required: deterrence and sufficient police resources to provide and follow up intelligence.

At present, targeting 'top-quality' drug traffickers is the job of the eight Regional Crime Squads outside London, and the Central Drugs Squad in the capital. Regional Crime Squads, which can cross force boundaries, became involved in drugs investigations in 1982 because, according to Derek Olley, 'In the course of their surveillance of top criminals they found that the criminals were becoming involved in drugs.' Intelligence is gathered and distributed by the Central Drugs Intelligence Unit at Scotland Yard, which is staffed by policemen from forces all over the country and customs officers. But there are not always enough men or time to follow up the intelligence properly. Derek Olley admits, 'We're doing nothing else but containing the problem. It's no good kidding ourselves.'

At last year's national police conference on drug abuse, police chiefs admitted they were not winning the war against dealers and decided to look into the idea of establishing nine regional drug squads. Barry Price, the drugs spokesman for the Association of Chief Police Officers, said that drug work was consuming so much of the existing Crime Squads' time that there was a danger that they could not get to grips with other investigations. His own personal and controversial view is that a national drug squad is needed: 'It is such a problem that we should swallow our distaste and local pride; it needs a national effort to knock off the big boys – they have international contacts and an awful lot of money. If I could have whatever I wanted, I would put a hundred first-class detectives to work at national level on getting stuck into the big boys.'

In July 1985 each regional crime squad was given a specialist drug force drawn from 200 officers. At the same time a national drugs intelligence unit staffed by police officers and customs men was set up, headed by Colin Hewett, the commander of Scotland Yard's Special Branch and anti-terrorist squad.

Deterrence is the other main plank of any strategy to fight major drug dealers. The government announced in October that it favoured legislation to increase the maximum penalty for trafficking in heroin from fourteen years to life imprisonment. Parole is now rarely given to drug traffickers sentenced to more than five years' imprisonment.

But the most important deterrent would be the power to seize all the profits a drug dealer has piled up from his trade. These profits are considerable. Michael Meacher, shadow spokesman for social services, wrote to *The Times* in 1984: 'As matters now stand, the profits of drug smugglers are widely rumoured to exceed in a single week the total amount of money allocated by the Department of

Health both to help existing addicts and deter others.' Derek Olley believes that, 'if we cannot take the profit out of drug trafficking, then we cannot stop it.'

But the law as it stands, cannot touch the real profits because it gives the courts the power to seize only assets that relate directly to the charge that is being heard. In the words of Olley, 'If you arrest someone with two kilos of heroin and £30,000 in his back pocket, he may have been dealing in heroin for five years – he may have a lovely house in Maidenhead, a yacht, two Rolls Royces in the drive, children at private school, a light aircraft at Biggin Hill – all accrued by drug dealing over a number of years. When he's arrested, if he doesn't admit anything except the two kilos and the thirty thousand pounds which he admits he's got from selling heroin, the court has the power to confiscate the thirty grand – but it can't touch his big house, the aeroplane, the cars, the yacht – because they're not related to the offence he's charged with.'

The police want this law changed. They want a fiscal investigation unit set up to investigate a suspected drug trafficker's assets as soon as he has been charged. They want a law under which the trafficker will have to prove that his money and possessions are not the fruits of drug trafficking – if he cannot, they will be seized as soon as he is convicted. Roy Penrose says: 'This will mean that a major drug trafficker sent down for nine to twelve years will not have the luxurious thought when he's sitting there in prison that he can come out one day to a multi-million-pound fortune.'

The fiscal investigation unit would bring together police, customs officers and Inland Revenue investigators into a multi-agency team. This approach has been tried with some success in the United States. In 1982, President Ronald Reagan announced new task forces involving, among others, the Internal Revenue Service, the Customs, the Bureau of Alcohol, Tobacco and Firearms, the FBI and the Drugs Enforcement Administration. The task forces have made great use of a statute which carries a maximum penalty of life imprisonment without parole, and provides for forfeiture of all proceeds from drug trafficking. Their 1984 Annual Report claimed considerable success: 'All (task forces) are producing polished significant cases, broad in scope with vertical penetration into significant trafficking organizations to a degree never previously achieved.'

Some sections of the British police would like to see the American system adopted forthwith. Others are more cautious. Earlier American efforts to control the heroin trade, despite massive law-enforcement campaigns' were signally ineffective, and the British are traditionally wary of such an approach. Roy Penrose says: 'Law enforcement alone will not solve the problem, that's the lesson we learnt from the USA. But on the other hand, we won't find a solution without law enforcement as an ingredient.'

The best way forward, he believes, is for police to join forces with the community and agencies that provide care in a 'multi-disciplinary approach'. He sees the current attempts at cooperation in the London Borough of Southwark, where the present 'heroin epidemic' was first highlighted, as a blueprint for the rest of the country.

Southwark now has a semi-permanent working-party whose job is to devise a strategy to control the supply and demand for heroin and other drugs in the borough. The police play a full role on this committee – along with all the other services that have anything to do with drugs – education, probation, youth social services, housing, health authorities, a street drug agency, two Drug Dependency Clinics and a Rehabilitation House. Judith Barker, a Southwark social worker who now coordinates the working-party says, 'There's no way we could do what we have to do without the police's help.'

She is the first to admit that Southwark has a long way to go. There are frequent disagreements and vast differences in approach. But without cooperation all parties in Southwark realize they have little chance of success: 'Because we've come into the problem very late ... there's no guarantee that the police will be 100 per cent successful in stopping the supply and we're not going to be 100 per cent successful in curbing demand. So we can't afford to get lost in conflict – that conflict would be lining the pockets of criminals,' says Barker.

It was the Bermondsey police who first alerted the local community to the number of children using drugs which were becoming increasingly available in September 1983. The Bermondsey Forum, a local community group, asked Barker to find out how big the problem was. She says that information from the police was invaluable for her assessment.

They produced their records of drug charges over six months and gave her the details of the type and amount of drug, and the postal code of where the charge was made. 'The information we collected was frightening. There was an awful lot more people than everyone suspected who were using skag (heroin) and many other drugs.'

At first, the police were inexperienced like everybody else and didn't know quite what to look for or what to do. But they soon developed a system. Dealers on the housing estates were to be handled by uniformed police and local CID. The Southwark District Crime Squad was to devote its energies to drug crimes and particularly to go for middle-level dealers, who are a vital part of the distribution chain, but often ignored. But Detective Inspector Dick Thompson believes this is not enough. 'If you just nick dealers they're replaced – that's not solving the problem. The police wanted to help addicts in other ways.'

Now the Southwark police would like to have a system to enable them to refer heroin users to advice-and-treatment centres early on in their drug-taking history. If a drug-user were arrested or cautioned, instead of being sent back out on the streets to take more drugs, they could be sent to trained and experienced counsellors for help: 'A referral system would require something like the Victims' Support Scheme to help victims of serious crime,' says Dick Thompson. If heroin addicts need more than counselling, the support workers would help them with practical problems like housing or send them to clinics and rehabilitation houses.

But for the multi-agency approach to become anything more than a talking-shop, money and more places for addicts to get help will have to be provided. It could be a long time before this happens – Southwark, like many other parts of the country, has financial problems because of rate-capping, and overcrowded hospitals and clinics. Dick Thompson says, 'In this area we have St Giles and Maudsley Hospitals and Phoenix House (a rehabilitation house) but they're already overwhelmed with customers from GPs and the probation services. Southwark police are keen to see a referral system, but at the moment we've got nothing to refer them to.'

[5] A compassionate health system?

'For those of us who have witnessed the rapid destruction of a loved one through drugs, within a society ill-equipped to treat and unconcerned about the problems of drug abuse, there exists a sense of despair towards a country that professes to have a compassionate health system.' So says a member of one of the many groups of anxious and frustrated parents throughout the country who have come together to fight for more and better facilities to treat drug users.

The spokesman of this group, Regional Emergency Aid for Addicts, is Patrick Monahan, a consultant surgeon in a Wiltshire hospital who discovered that there was no service in the area to help his daughter when she became a heroin addict: 'I was in a privileged position as a surgeon working for the NHS but even I couldn't get treatment. Immediate treatment for a drug addict is rarely available within the NHS.'

One mother described the nightmare she lived through trying to help her son who took an overdose of heroin: 'I spent twenty-four hours trying to get help for my son. It was a night and day of horror – I couldn't let my son out of my sight. The Royal Free Hospital in London discharged him, and at dawn he was staggering around the car park. He was semi-conscious and I was trying to phone everyone possible. I eventually was given a number by my doctor of an office in Charing Cross Road. But they could do no more than discuss the problem – there was nowhere to take him.' Her life started falling apart, along with her son's – 'I couldn't work, I couldn't sleep. I had to sell our house in Hampstead.'

Eventually her son did find some help: 'He was gradually weaned off at University College Hospital. But there was no back-up. He was detoxified but with no follow-up.' At first he appeared to be completely better, but two years later he relapsed and took another overdose. This time he died.

This tragedy highlights two serious flaws in Britain's provision for treating heroin addiction: too often no help at all is available; when it is available it is insufficient. Most of our hospitals can offer emergency help for addicts who have overdosed or, less commonly, two or three weeks' medical supervision and medication to help them 'withdraw' from the drug.

But when the physical dependence is cured, the addict still needs help for a psychological dependence, and counselling and therapy to deal with personal and social problems which heroin may have been masking – depression, loneliness, aggression, homelessness and unemployment are examples. This can be a long process requiring staff time, money, space and commitment. Why are these resources all too often in such limited supply?

Part of the answer lies in history. The foundation of treatment policy in Britain is the network of drug-dependence clinics which were set up to deal with the growing number of heroin addicts in the 1960s on the recommendation of the Brain Committee. They were designed to treat long-term 'junkies', many of them in their twenties, thirties and forties, by prescribing them a steady supply of drugs – heroin and cocaine at first, and later heroin substitutes such as methadone.

Intended to cater for an estimated 1000 addicts in the London area and a further 200 in the rest of the country, they have never been expanded and are now completely inadequate to deal with today's nationwide heroin epidemic which has affected perhaps fifty or one hundred times as many people, many of them young, potentially 'curable' and quite different from the clinics' traditional clientele.

The clinics did not come up to scratch even by the modest standards of the Brain Report which recommended in 1965 that drug-dependence units be set up both in and outside London as part of psychiatric hospitals or psychiatric wings of general hospitals. In fact while fourteen drug-dependency clinics were set up in the London area, less than a handful were established outside

London – where most addicts had to get treatment from the normal psychiatric services. Even today there are only seven proper drug clinics outside London (in England and Wales).

No blueprint for the ideal drug clinic was ever produced, but many of them did not even have the few basics suggested by the Brain Committee, which recommended: 'Each centre should have facilities for medical treatment, including laboratory investigation and provision for research.'

An important report *Treatment and Rehabilitation* published in 1982 by the Advisory Council on the Misuse of Drugs (which advises the government on ways to deal with the social problems arising from drug use) showed that hospital services for drug users vary wildly. 'Most provide out-patient clinics, which may or may not have access to laboratory services, including toxological services. A few have designated in-patient units but the majority are dependent on the availability of general psychiatric beds.' There are now only eighty-four beds set aside specifically for drug addicts in England and Wales, mostly in the London area, although there are 158 more in joint drug-and-alcohol wards.

Initially the clinics were funded centrally, by the government, because local bodies were not keen to provide money for such an unpopular group of patients. But after five years, central funding ran out and the clinics had to compete with other services for health authorities' scarce resources. Throughout the 1970s many of the clinics became run down as they lost social work and specialist medical staff.

Government attitudes to heroin abuse – that it was a self-inflicted illness – may have contributed to the clinics' decline. As recently as 1980, a senior Home Office official was quoted in the *Sunday Times* expressing opinions that would be frowned on in 1985: up to now, 'the aim has been rehabilitation ... but we can't afford this anymore. All we can do is to support these people for a time. But once they're hooked, they have effectively passed a death sentence on themselves.'

The same year Patrick Jenkin, the Secretary of State at the DHSS, told a meeting at Phoenix House, a drug rehabilitation house,

'While no one would for one moment question the value of the customs' surveillance of our ports or the police campaign against traffickers, it must be very evident to those in this hall that the same cannot always be said about the efforts to rehabilitate drug abusers.'

However, the available statistics do seem to show that some treatment is better than none. If heroin addicts are given no treatment at all, about 10 per cent will no longer be taking drugs after one year; this rises to 25 per cent after five years. Follow-up studies of British drug misusers attending clinics since 1968 show recovery rates significantly over the 'spontaneous' rate.

They also show that during the Seventies, a quarter to a third more opiate addicts in the UK were likely to be abstinent after five years than in Europe and the United States, possibly because of our out-patient drug-clinic system. Yet in 1980 Patrick Jenkin showed no commitment to strengthening our resources: 'I do not have to tell you that all this (treatment and research) is of course in competition with other more immediate and perhaps more obviously popular needs.'

The legacy of this London-centred approach to treatment and the subsequent years of neglect is today's patchy and inadequate system, unable to cope with the thousands of drug users seeking help in every part of the country.

Even London with its vastly superior clinics and full-time consultants in the drugs' field can hardly cope with the present crisis. The city's estimated 1000 addicts have mushroomed into 12,000 or 15,000 at the very least. London clinics commonly have waiting lists of up to two months just to interview patients and – where there are in-patient units – several months to give somebody a bed. Only four clinics in London have in-patient units. Other 'clinics' scarcely merit the name.

Hackney Drug Dependency Clinic consists of three small rooms and a cramped waiting-area in the semi-basement of an old Victorian workhouse. It has two social workers, a part-time doctor, John Mack, and a GP for three afternoons a week. It is supposed to cover five London boroughs with a total addict population of at least 2000. Dr Mack calls it a 'pathetic and pitiful service'. In 1983 there were four times as many people asking for treatment from the clinic as in 1980, and the numbers were still growing.

In 1984 the waiting-list for initial assessment of a patient was six to ten weeks and in June the clinic had to close its doors to new patients until January 1985. When the clinic re-opened it started to see over forty new patients a month. Dr Mack said, 'Our days are already filled and we have no time to go into the community or give advice to parents. We all go home with headaches, letters don't get answered, notes don't get written up.' But the clinic has now had promises of a consultant, a secretary and a nurse – the money to pay for them is from the DHSS and is only guaranteed for two years.

There is one hopeful development for London addicts – the National Temperance Hospital drug clinic, whose catchment area ranges from Soho to Tottenham, has plans to extend its service widely and open a day-programme for twenty to thirty addicts.

It will have a crèche, a kitchen with sufficient facilities to allow patients to make lunch every day and a number of new staff – a full-time psychologist, an occupational therapist, a clerical officer, two full-time family workers running the crèche and helping parents, two full-time nurses and extra medical sessions. Dr Martin Mitcheson, the consultant in charge of the clinic, says they hope to open satellite clinics or contact points in Soho, Haringey and Islington to get in touch with drug users who live far away from the clinic.

Outside London, National Health Services are even more stretched. Dr John Strang, in Manchester – *the only full-time drugs consultant outside London* – finds the imbalance shocking: 'London and the Home Counties have a network of specialist drug clinics. But when you move into the regions, there are virtually no specialist resources, with a much larger geographical area to be served.'

The seven drug-dependency clinics in the provinces that do exist are also fighting to keep their heads above water. Dr Ifti Akhter is a consultant psychiatrist who works in the twenty-seven-bed regional drug-and-alcohol unit in Birmingham. He has seen an explosion of new younger patients being referred at a rate of about forty a month, competing for the twenty-seven beds which have to be shared with about 1000 alcohol patients a year: 'We could double those twenty-seven beds and still find ourselves in difficulty. Since the Sixties, when we opened, there has only been a moderate expansion. We need more staff to cope.'

But Birmingham is probably one of the better services – All Saints' Hospital set up its addiction unit in 1964 and served as a model for the London clinics. It has managed to keep its waiting-list down and has now been given money from Birmingham City Council and the local health authority to expand its out-patient clinic.

The Standing Conference on Drug Abuse, has found that many parts of the country such as Cumbria, the North Midlands and most parts of the Home Counties have no NHS specialist services at all. Apart from the seven proper drug clinics, there are about sixteen centres which offer a skeletal, patchy service in England and Wales.

Scotland was taken completely by surprise by the heroin epidemic. Before 1980, it had a very small drug problem – and only one Edinburgh clinic and two Glasgow hospitals offered any sort of drug therapy. Between 1979 and 1983 the number of Scottish addicts trebled and there was a mad scramble to cope. Now six or seven hospitals in Glasgow will offer users help and a network of services is growing – but the Edinburgh clinic has closed. Wales has only one in-patient unit for the whole country. Throughout Britain, in-patient units are rare.

But the latest wave of heroin use has brought with it a question: Are drug dependency clinics the most appropriate form of help for Britain's young heroin users? When Darren, the 15-year-old Southwark addict mentioned in Chapter 3, was finally given an appointment to see a doctor at St Giles' Hospital in London, she refused to take him into the hospital, because he was only 15 and, she said, it would be bad for him to mix with hardened drug addicts.

One problem has always been that maintenance treatment is only suitable for a minority of drug addicts and it consumes a lot of the doctors' time. Most clinics are now moving away from long-term maintenance but they often still lack the staff to give time to young users who need intensive counselling and therapy. The addicts themselves are often unwilling to go to the clinics because of the stigma attached to psychiatric hospitals; others are not mature and stable enough to use them, and quickly drop out of treatment.

Druglink, the newsletter of the Institute for the Study of Drug Dependence, certainly passed a severe judgement on them in 1980: 'By and large, the clinics are fully occupied with the relatively settled old-timers, left over from the era of the old-time street junkie', and to some extent, 'they have become a backwater of our social response to drug abuse, dealing with a problem that no longer reaches the heart of the UK drug scene.'

This judgement was no doubt too harsh and hard-pressed doctors and nurses in the clinics have done their best to adapt treatment to the needs of younger users. But the limited resources at their disposal to treat an exploding addict population have certainly contributed to a great rise in the number of addicts who are going to their family doctors and private doctors for help.

In 1970, only 15 per cent of addicts notified to the Home Office were being treated by GPs or private doctors. By 1981 this had risen to 53 per cent, compared to 33 per cent being registered by treatment centres and 14 per cent by medical officers in the prison service.

Many heroin users go to their doctors because they prefer not to go to the clinics; Arthur Banks and Tom Waller in their booklet *Drug Addiction and Polydrug Abuse: the Role of the GP*, say, 'The addict may feel ashamed of his addiction as he would about VD and prefer a one-to-one relationship with the same doctor.' Others do not have the option of going to a clinic in any case.

Two Norfolk doctors, whose patients do not have access to a drug-dependency clinic, wrote to the *Sunday Times* to describe how they coped with this problem. 'My wife and I run a small country practice in Norfolk and have recently been horrified by the fact that we have three heroin addicts in our small village. We have sympathetic psychiatrists locally, but they have no facilities at all for dealing with this problem other than general wards, and our nearest units are Cambridge or Norwich which patients are unwilling and indeed, with the transport problems, are almost unable to get to.

'We have tried in our own inadequate way to help these folk and we think we have had success in helping one patient out of two off his addiction, although we realize that he may not be truly cured but notice he has not been coming to us for further supplies. As we are not specially licensed for heroin addicts we only use methadone and hope that this, together with weekly visits to us, and general support, will help them.'

But a lot of doctors are unwilling to take on drug users. Addicts can be difficult patients and doctors may not have the experience or training to cope with them. The booklet for GPs by Banks and Waller describes some of the pitfalls 'for the GP who decides to tread the inadequately charted minefield of addiction treatment'.

'The pressing need for renewal of the drug makes them among the most demanding and manipulative clients. They will use emotional blackmail and stress what suffering will occur to you if you do not prescribe . . . addicts have been charged for breaking into doctors' cars, drug cupboards and premises – so strengthen windows. At a lunch-hour they may wander into unguarded rooms looking for prescription pads lying about, so tighten your security . . . some of the stories addicts tell are extremely convincing, like that of the soldierly patient in a battledress "on leave from Northern Ireland", who recently obtained three prescriptions in one morning . . . with his tale of being hit by a tank.'

There is also the danger of isolated or elderly doctors yielding to threats of violence or blackmail and handing over whatever prescription the addict asks for. It is not surprising then that addicts divide doctors into two categories – those who don't want to know them and those who can be easily conned into giving out prescriptions to patients they don't know. Liberal prescribing by a handful of doctors was a major source of black market heroin in the 1960s. The problem does not exist on the same scale today; but NHS clinics are worried about one group of doctors who are prepared to take on drug addicts.

These are some private doctors who see hundreds of addicts daily in their plush consulting-rooms in Harley Street and Devonshire Place. They charge the addicts £30 for an appointment and prescribe a range of injectable and oral heroin substitutes.

The private doctors argue with some force that they have become necessary because what the NHS offers addicts is so little and so inappropriate. Dr Ann Dally, a leading champion of the private doctors working in the drug addiction field, says: 'Addicts don't like going to the clinics because they are often treated like dirt. They mix with hundreds of other addicts, which they don't like, they see different doctors every time they go – or sometimes they don't even see a doctor, but a nurse or a social worker instead.'

In June 1983, Thomas Bewley and Hamid Ghodse published a paper in the *British Medical Journal* claiming that private doctors were too easily persuaded to prescribe patients drugs such as diconal (a heroin substitute in tablet form which heroin addicts like to crush and inject) and ritalin (a central-nervous-system stimulant which prolongs the 'high' of diconal).

They warned that addicts turning away from the clinics and towards the private doctors who would freely prescribe heroin substitutes would lead to a severe spread of addiction. Bewley and Ghodse said that private doctors could make over £100,000 a year out of addiction and gave case histories to show that some of them prescribed drugs without making the proper checks on patients' histories.

There does seem to be some truth in this – one mother told the *Sunday Times* that her son died of an overdose as a result of careless prescribing by a private doctor. He went for an operation at a clinic in London's West End after he had been weaned off heroin. Immediately after he left the clinic, he walked across the road to the private doctor who used to supply him drugs, got himself a prescription and overdosed.

In 1982 and 1983 several of the private doctors were brought up before the General Medical Council for prescribing large amounts of injectable heroin substitutes without taking proper precautions. In 1982, Dr Nasir Ali Khan of Uxbridge was struck off for giving out diconal virtually on demand. He took on 350 drug addicts who paid him a £10 consultancy fee a time. Three of his patients died injecting themselves with a solution made from diconal. It then came to light that he had signed up to 10,000 private drug prescriptions in a year and probably made at least £100,000. The following year, Dr Desrath Rai of Harley Street was struck off the medical register for 'serious misconduct' after an addict he had prescribed diconal died of an overdose.

The test case was that case of Dr Dally, the President of the Association of Independent Doctors in Addiction, which the GMC heard in July 1983. She was being 'tried' for prescribing 105 tablets of diconal a week and some ritalin to a Coventry addict. The Council were told that she did check for new track marks on the addict's arms to satisfy herself that he would not inject diconal, but carried out no regular urine or blood tests to monitor his consumption of the drugs. She was found guilty of 'serious professional misconduct'.

But this did not serve the NHS doctors well in their case against the private doctors. Many doctors accused the GMC of using Dr Dally as a scapegoat – the evidence against her was not very strong and she was admonished rather than struck off. Dr Michael O'Donnell wrote in the *British Medical Journal* some weeks later: 'The impression left with observers who watched from the public gallery, and whose opinions have since been passed on and accepted in Whitehall, Fleet Street and ... even in Downing Street, is that a rigid and unimaginative medical establishment has impeached an idealistic doctor who had the cheek to question the party line on the management of drug addiction.'

The private doctors could also point to a survey done in the Seventies which confirmed that the clinics were every bit as guilty of 'irresponsible prescribing' as they. There was concern that primary methadone addicts were coming forward to the clinics – experienced addicts were selling the methadone they received from the clinics to young people and using the money to buy black-market heroin. The clinics were sure that this must be a result of general practitioners over-prescribing. But a Home Office survey of methadone prescribing in the London area showed beyond doubt that the major source of the surplus methadone was the clinics themselves.

Other correspondents to the *British Medical Journal* argued that while liberal prescribing of addictive drugs was not desirable, the problem should not be blown out of proportion. The main source of black-market drugs was Asia – the trickle of drugs that leaked from both the clinics and the private doctors was insignificant by comparison. All efforts should now be directed to helping the victims of international drug trafficking.

Nevertheless, the solution to the 'private doctor problem' suggested in Bewley and Ghodse's paper was readily taken up by other clinic doctors – to extend the licensing system that already exists for doctors prescribing heroin and cocaine to all controlled drugs. They drummed up a lot of influential support and in April 1984 the government announced that only doctors specially licensed by the Home Office were to prescribe diconal to addicts.

Later that year, a working-party of doctors set up by the DHSS after the *Treatment and Rehabilitation* report in 1982 recommended secretly to the government that all heroin substitutes except for oral methadone, which is commonly used to wean someone gradually off heroin, should be licensed in the same way.

If the government favours this extension of licensing, it will also strengthen the hand of those who argue that the maintenance of addicts with narcotic drugs is bad treatment. This is a debate that has raged since the drug clinics were set up in 1968. The clinics were given the power to give out addictive drugs not only for medical, but also for social reasons. The policy-makers believed that giving addicts a regular supply of 'clean' drugs under the supervision of a doctor would stabilize their lives; their health would improve, they could hold down jobs, bring up families and avoid contact with criminal activity.

The other non-medical aim of long-term prescribing was to hold the black market in check by providing a cheaper, cleaner alternative source of drugs. For a few years, this policy seemed to be working. The number of 'junkies' taking heroin appeared to stabilize as they flocked to the clinics to get their prescriptions, first of heroin and later of methadone. Helen McKay, a 31-year-old woman from Edinburgh, was one of those for whom the system seems to work. She became a heroin addict at 21 after her husband died in a car crash. Her life quickly became grim: 'searching the streets for heroin'.

Then six-and-a-half years ago, she started going to the Royal Edinburgh Hospital where she would collect her weekly prescription of twenty-four tablets of methadone a day. She saw the clinic as a lifeline and a way to maintain a stable home for her 11-year-old son. 'At least you know where you are with a regular prescription. I couldn't go back to how I used to live ... I stay clean and out of trouble through this prescription, and I don't want to start anything else at this stage. I'm quite happy and stable. I just want to be able to live in peace.'

But then her stability and peace were threatened. The Royal Edinburgh Hospital closed its one-day-a-week clinic for prescribing methadone in February 1985. This was partly due to lack of funds; but the clinic became a target for 'cuts' because of the growing school of thought in clinics all over the country against prescribing addictive drugs. It began in the 1970s as doctors became frustrated at having to act like 'policemen with white coats on'. Their prescribing methods might be regulating drug use, but they weren't 'curing their patients'.

As Dr John Mack of Hackney Drug Clinic put it: 'Very few people would feel that giving alcohol to an alcoholic was treatment – but it's surprising how many people would argue that giving narcotics to a drug addict is treatment.' Another consultant, quoted in the book *Heroin Addiction: Treatment and Control in Britain* by G. Stimson and E. Oppenheim, said, 'I hate admitting that anybody's being maintained because I think that if one openly declares that you're running a maintenance programme for anybody then it's so easy just to stop talking to them, and stop caring about people and stop helping them over crises and stop doing any supportive case-work, it's so easy just to opt out of that and say, "Well, there's your ration-book, show your face every couple of weeks and if you're not dead you carry on drawing it".'

Two studies carried out in the Seventies, one at University College Hospital in London and the other at the Southern General Hospital in Glasgow, added fuel to this argument. The UCH study by Dr Martin Mitcheson and Richard Hartnoll showed that there was little difference in health, employment and drug use between people being prescribed heroin and others getting oral methadone.

Methadone had been discovered in Germany in the Thirties and was introduced as a replacement for heroin in America in the 1960s – its advantage was that, unlike heroin, one dose of methadone a day was sufficient and it didn't have to be injected. At the time of the study, many clinics started prescribing their addicts methadone instead of heroin; the change was seen as a way of patients 'confronting' their drugs problem.

The Glasgow study of 1978 took the argument a stage further. It compared a group of illicit heroin users with a group being maintained on methadone. It concluded: 'Our comparison ... does not support many of the claims made for drug maintenance. Most of the maintenance group continued to use illicit drugs. We did not find that methadone was necessary to maintain treatment contact. We found no significant difference in the numbers employed in the two groups.'

In 1983, the Southern General Hospital decided to cease prescribing methadone and set up a Drug Stopping Clinic to encourage people to stop taking drugs. Patrick Mullen, the consultant psychiatrist who runs the clinic, believes that giving out methadone is inappropriate for the very young population with short drug-taking careers who now come to the clinic.

By refusing to dole out drugs, the clinic is trying to dispel the myth that you need to take drugs to stop drugs. Mullen says that in any case it would be almost impossible now to arrange a 'dishing-out' service for Britain's 50,000 or more heroin addicts – the risk of giving heroin to non-addicts or ex-addicts would be very high.

But despite the obvious logic of the arguments against long-term prescribing as an effective treatment, the proposal to allow only licensed doctors to prescribe drugs and substitutes to addicts is severely opposed by many in the drug field who want to encourage

GPs to stay involved with heroin addicts. They say that the drawback with licensing is that it would restrict GPs' involvement in heroin treatment; most of the licences would go to the hospital clinic doctors and not to GPs.

Until the poorly funded clinics have vastly expanded and developed policies to attract the majority of drug-users, most drug-takers will be left with no treatment at all if GPs are not encouraged to treat them. One drug expert in the voluntary sector is exasperated that this measure (licensing) would be a diversion from the task facing family doctors, social workers, clinics and independent doctors to come together and find the best possible policies for the future: 'What's happening is that a private battle between a number of NHS doctors in London and some private doctors has been made into a matter of principle when it isn't. I tend to think "A plague on both their houses". The private doctors are foolish because they have not tried to work in tandem with drug-treatment centres. The drug-treatment centres have not allowed the partnership to develop. The only people who suffer are the drug users.'

Dr Arthur Banks, a Chelmsford doctor working in an area where there is no nearby clinic, and a champion of the theory that general practitioners should get involved with heroin users, says that further licensing would be a 'draconian measure' and 'a sledge-hammer to crack a nut'. All GPs would be penalized for the misbehaviour of a few. Licensing would suspend doctors' rights to clinical judgement by forcing most doctors to use oral methadone. This would deter doctors from taking addicts as patients: they would assume that there was nothing useful they could do.

Yet in the present woefully inadequate treatment system, GPs will doubtless have to carry a larger and larger burden. They will have to assume it with little back-up, little training, no extra payment and possibly an official deterrent if licensing is extended. Instead of discouragement, GPs should be getting training on hospital courses. Drug-dependency clinics should be offering them support, training and laboratory facilities wherever possible. Dr Roy Robertson, an Edinburgh GP, says that his practice has more than one hundred drug users on its books because the regional drug-treatment centre does not offer a service for the new wave of young users. But, he says, they need more resources for things like urine testing to do the job properly: 'If there were hospital-based enthusiasm for it, things would be easier for us.'

So with drug clinics overburdened and unable to cope, and other doctors unwilling, untrained or discouraged from taking on heroin addicts, it is little wonder that the burden falls on other parts of the system. Sooner or later, heroin addicts who haven't been able to get treatment come into conflict with the law. Indeed a Manchester drug centre, Lifeline, has said, 'Prison continues to be the major resource for the "treatment" of the majority of drug users in this country.' For the lucky ones, prison – or help from the probation services – will lead to withdrawal from heroin and possibly a 'cure'. But is prison the best place to wean an addict off heroin?

Robert, an ex-addict who wrote to the *Sunday Times* from prison, considers himself 'one of a lucky minority' for whom prison was the necessary jolt out of a life which revolved around drugs. 'I am aged 32 and, up until my reception into prison, I had a drug problem for a number of years. My addiction to heroin started in the same way as it has for many others . . . by the occasional "snort" and "smoke" . . . My addiction soon became a full-time occupation. I lived for my next crank.

'A friend, who was also in the same mess, and I robbed a chemist shop and tied up the occupants, and made off with the contents of the drug cabinet. We went wild with our cache and increased our addiction to an enormous level . . . Ten months after doing the chemist robbery, the law caught up with us . . . I was almost at the cemetery gate and my pal was even closer. He was about ten years younger, had been rushed into hospital, and had suffered a stroke and renal failure. He had also had pneumonia and blood poisoning . . . it was a miracle he pulled through.

'We were sentenced to three years' imprisonment and are now almost half-way through our second year. He is in a different prison and we are no longer in contact with each other. When I get out of here, I am going to a rehabilitation centre for ex-drug addicts. I am going to rebuild my life and keep away from the smack scene.

I am one of the small minority who have managed to finally escape from the snares of heroin addiction.'

Parents often see a prison sentence for their son or daughter as a last hope – especially if they have been sent from pillar to post by the treatment services looking in vain for some help. When the mother of Darren, the young Southwark addict, found out that her son was taking heroin, she became determined to get him away from the housing estate, away from his friends and dealers. She went straight to the emergency department at Guy's Hospital and was told to take Darren to see a GP. 'The GP wasn't much help, he just talked about religion,' she said. 'He said that if we had lived the ways of the Lord, that this would never have happened.'

The Samaritans – she telephoned everybody she could think of – told her there was a drug-addiction unit at Guy's. So she went back to the hospital and was told she'd need a letter of referral. Growing desperate, she at last got an appointment at St Giles', the local hospital – but not for six weeks. Things were getting so bad that she went back to the casualty department at Guy's. They told her to wait for her St Giles' appointment.

'Finally we got to see the doctor in March. She talked to Darren first of all, and he came storming out, said it was a waste of time. She wouldn't give him an alternative drug which he thought he'd get, a liquid substitute. She said he'd have to come and see her regularly first of all ... I thought the hospital would solve everything. But you talk and talk and never seem to get anywhere.'

Without treatment, it was inevitable that Darren was going to get into trouble. He was stealing to pay for his 'skag' and so he was arrested several times. Each time he was let off: 'It was no good. There was nowhere to send him. It was just like going to court for a day out. The police would charge him and then the courts would let him out.' But eventually he was sent to a detention centre for three months.

In the centre, he stopped taking heroin, put on weight and came out looking fit and healthy. At first he stayed with his mother and father in other areas of London where there was less of a drug problem: he said he could not stay in Southwark because 'so many people are out to get me for the thefts, and all the kids that are still on it are trying to get hold of me to join them again.' The family were full of new hope and his father promised to get him a job in the scaffolding trade after his eighteenth birthday. Darren told his parents, 'All I want to do now is to enjoy myself, get some new clothes and a new job.'

But the story did not have a happy ending. After eight months he did not have a job and showed all the signs of being back on heroin. He returned to Southwark and got in touch with his old friends. He looked ill and thin and was constantly demanding money. His mother said, 'He's getting very aggressive again. He can't settle and can't accept the way life is.' Detention gave Darren a break from heroin but it did not teach him how to change his life.

Several studies have shown that, in most cases, prison does not help addicts to stay off drugs. Most British prisons do not offer help or counselling to drug offenders who may go through traumatic withdrawals in prison with no support. Those which do – including Holloway, Wormwood Scrubs and Pentonville – can offer only limited help. At present, Holloway's therapeutic unit can offer special facilities for only six addicts, and is threatened with closure.

The most convincing evidence that prison is bad for addicts is in the heroin overdose figures: 10 per cent of people who die from heroin overdoses do so after coming out of prison. They do not realize that their tolerance to the drug has been reduced by their forced withdrawal and go straight back to the level of dose they were taking before.

For those who survive, the probation and after-care service is a major source of advice and support, especially outside London where other services are so thin on the ground. A Parole Release Scheme has been set up in the voluntary sector to try and put drug offenders released on parole in touch with agencies that can help them. The probation service may provide merely counselling or sometimes a place in one of their hostels, which may offer some sort of rehabilitation.

Generally, however, probation service hostels and day-centres insist on their clients being drug-free and cannot offer any treatment. Some probation officers have developed links with street agencies and rehabilitation projects and the service has provided staff for hostels. But at present the help they can give to drug users is limited – probation officers get very little training to deal with drug misuse. Mr S. Ratcliffe of the Inner London Probation Service says, 'If the probation service is one of the front-line organizations for drug users then it's poorly prepared – it's not been a very substantial part of our officers' training.'

He warns that, 'The probation services cannot be all things to all men.' He would like them to have more drug training so that they can advise drug addicts in their care on what to do and who can help them: 'I don't want the probation service to do much more – I would like it to have access to more helping agencies.' This cry is voiced over and over again by agencies who are ready and willing to help addicts find treatment, but discover that there is little help to be found.

If prison does not work, the NHS specialist drug-treatment centres cannot cope, and other agencies have little to offer, could an ideal treatment system exist? Gradually society is beginning to realize, to the relief of some doctors, that drug abuse is not just a problem for the medical profession, although access to basic medical treatment for every drug user should be the core of any system. One drug-clinic doctor said that the assumption that it was purely a 'doctor's dilemma' let everyone else off the hook. Now there is a general acceptance that there is no easy answer – and everybody has to take part in the fight against heroin addiction.

The Advisory Council for the Misuse of Drugs put forward suggestions for the ideal form of treatment in its 1982 report which were widely supported: 'There is no typical addict, it follows that there is no single treatment or rehabilitation strategy confined to one discipline or service which will be effective for all individuals. Each individual drug misuser's problems must be assessed and the most appropriate match made to the services available.' This approach draws in the skills of doctors, social workers, probation officers, teachers and health educators. 'The need for the various disciplines to recognize each other's skills and contributions and to improve collaboration becomes paramount.'

Sadly, three years on, the ideal 'multi-disciplinary' approach has rarely been achieved. Doctors do not see eye to eye with each other; most health authorities do not have the will or the money to coordinate a network of services for drug users; the government 'strategy' has done something to help, but not enough.

The North-West Region of England, however, is a shining light in the wilderness. There, thanks to the tireless efforts of Dr John Strang, the consultant in charge of the drugs clinic at Manchester's Prestwich Hospital and his colleagues, district drug teams are being set up throughout the Region and the in-patient unit is being expanded from six to twenty beds.

Dr Strang and his small team treat six heroin addicts in a grim Victorian building opposite a huge black chimney in the grounds of Prestwich Hospital. Inside it is homely and comfortable, though spartan, and the patients are grateful to be there.

For a century, Prestwich has been known as the local asylum, so Dr Strang is campaigning to have the unit moved out of the hospital into the community, rather than build an extension. 'However glossy the extension, the local stigma remains,' he said. Drug addicts will stay in the new unit for two or three months with decreasing supervision: 'Before they leave they could be living in a self-contained flatlet. They would come into the in-patient unit in the daytime, but cook for themselves and keep themselves and the flat clean in the evening. They will become increasingly self-sufficient. For example, they could be out job-hunting or flat-hunting in Rochdale and trying to form healthy attachments in their last month here.'

Geographically the unit is close to the centre of the Region's drugs-treatment network. But it is only one of the options for treating the more than 1000 drug addicts who look for help in the north-west each year. A two to three months' period of treatment was chosen for the unit – to fill a gap. 'Addicts can have two to three weeks in a local hospital to dry out, with community support from the local drugs team. If this is insufficient, the next step up is a year in a rehabilitation house. That's a huge step, particularly if you have children. The unit will offer something between the two,' says Dr Strang.

There are strong links between the Regional Drug Clinic and the new community drug teams – five of which are already working while at least seven more have been funded. John Strang and two specialist nurses travel from Blackpool to Rochdale to Salford holding drugs treatment and counselling sessions wherever districts are willing to provide space. The drug teams, usually consisting of three full-time workers, are based in health or community centres. Dr Strang says the crucial thing about them is: 'They are not the entire service, they act as local agents provocateurs – they are the key which opens the doors to general-hospital beds ... They are the Dr Kissingers of the drugs service. They have the links with local GPs, adult education, housing departments, they can persuade local polytechnics to take on ex-drug addicts. They must be a full-time committed team to bring about a change in the whole fabric of services.'

All this has been made possible by one thing – local money. In 1985 the Regional Health Authority voted a large, permanent slice of Regional Development funds to be allocated to districts for use in the drugs field and invited bids for local projects. This would seem to vindicate the government's policy of providing three years' central funding to get drug projects started, to be taken over by local funds when government money runs out.

The government has allocated £10 million in England and £2 million in Scotland over three years for treatment projects in the National Health Service and the voluntary sector. Only in Wales is the long term accounted for, as the Welsh Office has offered to provide continuing funding for certain drug projects. Cardiff has been given £50,000 revenue a year to set up a day-centre.

However, so far, no other regions have shown any sign of following the north-west's example. Health authorities clearly do feel the need for better drug services: when the government put forward its first offer of pump-priming money, one region put in bids for more than half the sum available for everybody. But most districts say they don't have the money in their own coffers to support services when the government money runs out.

Dr Strang emphasizes the importance of drug projects having

stability: 'The sad reality of most central funding is that it's one-off, like winning the pools. When that's gone, you're back to where you were. It's vital that services can survive when drugs are no longer "flavour of the year".' A director of social services said, 'Ten million pounds pump-priming money ... is welcome, but the problem is where money would come from once the pump is primed.' If health authorities cannot afford it, neither can local authorities – whose spending powers are being reduced by government penalties, rate-capping and the abolition of metropolitan councils.

It is ironic that the Advisory Council for the Misuse of Drugs, which first proposed the multi-disciplinary approach, failed to recommend the tool most needed to achieve it – permanent central funding. Brian Pearson, a Standing Conference on Drug Abuse agency's field-worker, called it, 'A spectacular failure of nerve.' The *Lancet* in 1983 said prophetically, 'The trouble with such proposals ... is that it is all too easy for government departments to accept them and yet for regions and districts to do nothing about them.'

Three years after the Advisory Council's report, there has been a proliferation of working-parties and conferences, of circulars and questionnaires from the DHSS and replies from health authorities, of publicity about government money and government strategies. Yet services for drug users have hardly expanded at all.

The belief of many drug experts that the DHSS has tried to solve the problem on the cheap seems to be borne out by its own press release in February 1984: 'The Report points to a way forward that does not depend upon the creation of costly new institutions.' Pearson also noted: 'This government has spent more time on the problem than any previous government, but it has largely been a cosmetic exercise. I sometimes think the government would do anything to stamp out the drug problem, as long as it doesn't involve spending too much money.'

[6]   No magic cures

Much of the help and advice that is available to heroin addicts comes from committed voluntary organizations that have been formed in response to the gaping holes in NHS services. Although many of them are already operating on a shoestring, their financial future may become even more bleak as they are squeezed by government cutbacks. Yet they offer a wealth of experience and expertise in the thinly populated field of advice, counselling and rehabilitation services for addicts.

Some of the voluntary services have been going since the mid-Sixties, when they were set up in response to the growing problem of rootless, drifting heroin users converging on London's West End. The first of these organizations, like the Community Drugs Project in Camberwell, and the Blenheim Project in west London, offered advice and day-care facilities. After the hospital drug-treatment clinics were established in the late Sixties, it became clear that although an addict could be helped by treatment to give up drugs, there was nowhere to help them stay off. Getting rid of their physical dependence on the drug did not help solve the problems that led people to heroin in the first place.

In 1968, the Advisory Committee on Drug Dependence re-commended that rehabilitation hostels should be set up, which would make addicts sort out their chaotic lives – but this national system never got off the ground. Once again, voluntary groups stepped into the breach, with a scattered development of services. A couple of rehabilitation houses run by evangelical Christians were already in existence, and voluntary organizations began to set up a few other rehabilitation centres, such as Phoenix House, in south London.

The number of rehabilitation communities has now grown from

four or five in 1970 to about nineteen. By the end of 1985, there will be about 500 places – a rise from only 380 in 1982. On top of that, there are another seventy places or so in private, fee-paying rehabilitation units.

The street counselling and advice services have also grown. Many are run by volunteers, and have been very important in demanding recognition that heroin addiction is an escalating problem.

Despite the fact that they provide essential services, nearly all of these voluntary organizations are beset with funding problems. The 1982 report of the Advisory Council on the Misuse of Drugs, was concerned about the lack of money for services that were already overstretched: 'The failure to provide adequate funds can only result in the piecemeal development of services in response to crises, rather than in planned and coordinated development.

'The non-statutory agencies involved in treatment and rehabilitation rely on an insecure combination of local and central government funding and exist under the constant threat of financial collapse.'

The £10 million offered by the DHSS was heavily over-subscribed, and was inevitably spread thinly amongst the many voluntary organizations that needed help. An additional frustration for the services competing for a slice of the cake was that the money was for new projects, rather than for existing ones. As one administrator put it: 'It's an Alice in Wonderland situation. You end up inventing new projects, in the hope of getting some money, when you can't even keep your present ones from going under.'

The abolition of the GLC and the Metropolitan Councils will add to the looming problems, as many voluntary organizations rely on grants from them in order to survive. David Turner, coordinator of the SCODA, points out: 'The problem of funding is not going to go away. Services are faced with a perpetual funding crisis – and it takes very little for them to be confronted with the final straw that breaks the camel's back.'

The Blenheim Project, which offers advice, information and counselling to drug users and their families, is one of the oldest and most established street agencies. Its work is more in demand than ever before – in 1984 it saw 2647 people, an increase of almost 700 on the year before. The project also encouraged many women to come and get help – as they are often overlooked, or reluctant to admit that they have a problem. Yet despite the value of its work, the project is continually struggling to keep its head above water. Its £7500 annual grant from the DHSS ended in April 1985, and at the same time a £14,000 GLC grant looked shaky because of the scheduled abolition of the Council.

The Community Drug Project, a counselling and education service in south London, faces the same problems. In 1984 the DHSS withdrew its annual grant of £5000 – suggesting that the Regional Health Authorities might care to pick up this bill, along with that of the Blenheim Project. CDP's annual grant from the GLC, which paid for the wages of one of its counselling workers and a quarter of the running costs, also looked uncertain. These financial worries were the last thing the project needed, when they had to cope with hundreds of young heroin addicts, from the nearby estates of Southwark and Bermondsey.

Even when a voluntary organization offers a unique service, its future is not always secure. City Roads Crisis Intervention Centre, in north London, is the only place that will take young addicts when they have nowhere else to go, treat them to get drugs out of their system, and gives them three weeks of advice, care and encouragement to accept long-term help. The centre has lurched from one financial crisis to another – and by the spring of 1985, City Roads faced a deficit of £75,000. Its services were in huge demand, with admissions up 30 per cent since the beginning of 1985, and a doubling of referrals in two years. In 1984 the centre offered about 300 addicts residential places, in its hostel in a shabby Islington street, out of the 1200 people referred there.

For Barry, a 27-year-old addict who was admitted to the centre in December 1984, City Roads was a last resort: 'If it wasn't for this place, I think I'd be dead. I was desperate. I'd tried to get help in clinics in London and Manchester, but I was rejected and told to come back in eight months. I know it wasn't their fault, but you start thinking they're pushing you to see how far you can go. If I hadn't been accepted here, I'd have taken an overdose.'

Although City Roads is London-based, it is often the final hope for people who have drifted to the capital from all over the country. Some of them will have been sleeping rough, and many are on the verge of overdosing once too often. The centre's DHSS grant came to an end in April 1985, and the four hard-pressed London Regional Health Authorities were supposed to take over funding. Giampi Alhadeff, the energetic director of City Roads, is increasingly caught up in a search for money: 'We have been working for seven years, and have a wealth of knowledge and experience – so the least we deserve is the security of knowing we will continue to exist, and not have to worry from week to week about money.'

These money problems came at a time when the centre was hoping to expand. It had raised money from charity to buy the crumbling Georgian house next door, but was unsure where to find the £120,000 to renovate it. The extra space was badly needed for training, counselling and to provide facilities for women who wanted to bring their children in with them while they had treatment. City Roads is particularly keen to be able to help more women, as many more are becoming heroin addicts than before, without adding the pressure of putting their children into care. In a couple of months since the end of 1984, the centre treated five women using heroin from one estate in east London alone – all of whom had to leave their children whilst at City Roads.

But any innovations continue to have a shadow cast over them. Dennis Muirhead, chairman of the management committee of City Roads, is angry about the waste of time and effort in scrambling for funds: 'In business terms we're nutters – we have to work with a deficit every year, and it feels very scary.'

Many of the long-term rehabilitation houses run by voluntary organizations, face similar funding problems, that hang over them from day to day. Stillwaters, a rehabilitation house for eight addicts in Nevendon, Essex, is run by Ruth and Ian Law as an extended family. Their budget is so slim that the Laws receive no salary at all. At the beginning of April 1985, the lease on the house, an old rectory owned by the diocese of Chelmsford, ended and there was no foreseeable prospect of the Laws being able to buy it. They had applied to the DHSS in August 1984 for a grant of £125,000, to be able to buy the house, and were still waiting for an answer from the department.

Ruth Law was still hoping for a promise of help from the DHSS, while the house was operating on borrowed time from the diocese in April: 'But if we don't get the money, and no fairy godmother steps in, we'll be shattered – and very angry,' she said. 'We've got six residents in here at the moment – where are we supposed to go?'

Although Stillwaters is small, it is vital for many addicts who have been helped by its caring family atmosphere. Ruth Law points out that 75 per cent of the people who go there have already been to the larger rehabilitation houses, which have not been able to help them: 'We've got no magic cures here, but some people find our set-up suits them better. We've got our place, but the DHSS don't seem to care. We're trying to keep a good face on things, hoping something will turn up, but it's very hard.'

Not all rehabilitation houses have the same immediate financial problems. Phoenix House, established in 1970, had expanded from its original London base with the help of DHSS grants. In May 1984 a second Phoenix House was opened in Sheffield, with money from the initiative scheme for new projects. With one hundred addicts referred there within seven months of its opening, it quickly filled its thirty beds. Another Phoenix House opened in 1985 in South Tyneside, despite local opposition, and the organization hopes to be able to find the money for a rehabilitation hostel in the Wirral. Unfortunately the DHSS grants will only last three years, after which time alternative funding has to be found from local authorities – some of whom may be very short of cash.

Phoenix House is a 'concept house', which means that residents work their way up a hierarchical structure. It hopes to restore the self-discipline and self-respect that addicts have lost – and to help them try to understand and solve the reasons why the addiction has taken hold. People are required to stay for up to twelve months and are expected to help run the house, and take part in intensive group sessions. The Phoenix House philosophy states: 'Here at last we can appear clearly to ourselves, not as the giant of our dreams, nor the dwarf of our fears, but as part of the whole, with a share in its purpose. Here together we can take root and grow, not alone as in death but alive in ourselves and in others.'

The first Phoenix House is in a rambling Victorian villa in the south London suburb of Forest Hill. It has places for fifty-six people, with another twelve in a halfway hostel. Like City Roads, Phoenix House would like to be able to offer much more help to addicts with children, and is hoping to convert a derelict house in the grounds into a family unit in 1985.

Although Phoenix House is not faced with financial disaster, it is straining to meet the demand for treatment. In the first three weeks of 1985, the London Phoenix House had to turn away seventy people – and could only offer five places. David Tomlinson, the executive director, has tried to accommodate the increasing pressure on Phoenix House: 'Demand is becoming very high. We have had to limit our catchment area to Greater London – but we get requests for help from all over the country. There just aren't the resources for everybody. More and more people need the service. We're not yet getting the 12 to 16-year olds – but imagine the pressure in five years when we start picking them up.'

He does not believe there is much point in having a waiting-list, because addicts tend to drift away and disappear before they can be helped. Tomlinson is sure that 'if we really wanted to face up to the degree of need in this country, we would have to have a major expansion'.

He is echoed by people trying to provide rehabilitation services throughout the country. Bridge House was set up in Bradford in the summer of 1984 to provide five beds for people who have been detoxified, and need time and space to work out what to do next. By the spring of 1985, it was clear that many more people needed the service than there was room for, as it covered the huge area of the Yorkshire Ridings single-handed. In March alone, the voluntary organization that ran Bridge House was concerned that it had been forced to postpone four people's entry into the hostel, with the prospect of a six-week wait before there would be room. The project was hoping that it could move into a larger house, and take ten or twelve people to ease the pressure.

In Surrey, the Cranstoun Project has to turn away three or four people a week who want to come into its rehabilitation house, because there simply is not enough room. The project can offer only nine places to men between the ages of 18 and 35, and they stay from nine to twelve months. Some come from detoxification units, some from home and some from prison. Like other rehabilitation houses, the residents are expected to be drug-free on arrival and throughout their stay. The funding comes from each resident's local authority – although some will not pay up.

There are three stages in the rehabilitation programme at Cranstoun. The men move through each one, with more responsibility as they progress, after an assessment and vote by the whole house. Everyone has cooking and cleaning jobs to do, and on weekdays they have three hours of group therapy, when they are encouraged to talk about their problems. They also mix with the surrounding community, and some of the men do part-time work like painting and gardening for local people. For Malcolm, who came to Cranstoun in the middle of 1984, it was the first place that had helped him stay off drugs in the ten years he had been using them since the age of 16: 'When I arrived at Cranstoun, I expected to be told how to come off drugs, but in fact all the work comes from you. You don't want to hear the truth about yourself, but here you come to understand your strengths and weaknesses, and what makes you want to use drugs. And I like the friendships you make – everyone looks after each other.'

Malcolm was one of the lucky ones, managing to get a place at Cranstoun after a five-month sentence in Pentonville prison. Many heroin addicts, even if they have the motivation to ask for long-term help, cannot find a place. In a study of eight rehabilitation houses, undertaken in 1980 for the Advisory Council on the Misuse of Drugs, four out of every five applicants were unsuccessful in gaining admission. The main reasons given for not accepting a suitable candidate were that there was no room, or the applicant was sent to prison, or there were difficulties in getting the funding for a resident.

But for those people who are able to afford private fees, queues can be jumped. The Priory Hospital in Roehampton, south-west London, is a splendid Gothic Building nestling between a golf course and the Bank of England sports grounds. This private psychiatric hospital has the atmosphere of a comfortable, discreet hotel, with single rooms decorated in pastel colours, mostly with their own bathroom. A standard room costs £145 a day, and extra is charged for consultants' fees and tests. A deposit of £1000 has to be paid.

There is no set time that heroin addicts stay, but it tends to be about a month. If an addict is accepted by the Priory, after referral from a doctor, they will be given a methadone detoxification programme for one or two weeks. If this is successful, the next phase of the treatment uses relaxation techniques, psychotherapy, bio-feedback machines and physical education. Each patient is watched over by a team of nurses and a consultant, and they also have a self-help group.

Rebecca was sent to the Priory by her parents in 1983, when she was 20, after failing to give up heroin by herself. Her first visit there lasted ten days: 'For the first four days I was alone, just seeing a few nurses. They use a black box for physical side effects when you're withdrawing – it gives you electrical currents behind your ears, which are supposed to take your mind off the other pains. I got hysterical on my third day, and ripped the black box off and threw it at the window. I just wanted to die. I couldn't get out because all the doors were locked, and they gave me a large dose of sedative.' For the rest of her stay she saw a doctor every day: 'We just talked about how I was feeling.'

Rebecca did not take heroin for five months after leaving the Priory: 'but then I blew it. I had a blitz one weekend, and I felt so sad, I phoned to ask my mother for help. I went back to the Priory for three days, but when I came out I started using heroin again, so I went back to the Priory for another week. It just seemed to trickle on and on.'

By 1984 she felt sure she had given up heroin, partly because of her own determination: 'I think the success of the Priory totally depends on the person involved – if you go there wanting to stop, you'll be cured.'

The Priory sends some of its more intransigent patients to Broadway Lodge, a former convent on the outskirts of Weston-Super-Mare. This rehabilitation house is run as a charity, but two thirds of the places are for fee-paying patients, who are charged £665 a week. For about a third of the patients the fees are waived, if they cannot afford them, but they are asked to pay back £1000 if and when they start earning again after leaving Broadway Lodge.

Broadway Lodge was set up in 1975, and based on a form of treatment called the Hazelden method, or the Minnesota model, first developed in 1949 in America at the Hazelden Foundation in Minnesota. Its basic tenet is that heroin addiction is not an illness, nor a crime, and is no different from alcoholism or dependence on any other drug. As one of its disciples puts it: 'Addicts are to be treated as sick people trying to get well, rather than bad people trying to get good.'

The Lodge houses about forty-one addicts and alcoholics at a time, and has a comfortable, easygoing atmosphere. Heroin addicts are weaned off the drug within three to seven days, and most of them find the experience no worse than 'uncomfortable' or a 'bad dose of flu'. Staying off is harder, and most patients need to remain at Broadway Lodge for at least eight weeks – and some stay a year.

However long it takes, the success rate has proved remarkably high. The key to the treatment is that patients are supposed to help each other, and most of the counsellors are also former addicts. The principle is simple. Addicts will lie even to themselves about their determination to give up drugs. But, in the words of one former patient who went to Broadway Lodge after conventional, unsuccessful treatment at a London clinic: 'It's hard to lie to another junkie – they can see right through you.'

Hetty, a 25-year-old ex-heroin addict, is a shining success story for Broadway Lodge. She had been using drugs since the age of 15, and had a series of disastrous treatments at various clinics and hospitals up and down the country. Eventually she ended up in Broadway Lodge, paid for by her desperate parents: 'When I first arrived at Broadway, I didn't believe them when they told me I was an addict. I thought they were all very strange, like a weird sect, and felt like I was having a nervous breakdown.

'We were made to talk to each other about our experiences – and it took me about six months to accept that I was an addict.' She still has reservations about Broadway Lodge, and thinks that its rehabilitation programme has its drawbacks: 'By the end of my stay, when I had worked my way up the hierarchy, it was like being top of the school, and I was as horrible as possible to new people. My motives certainly weren't to help them.

'Then I went to the half-way house in Weston-Super-Mare, where there were eight girls. I was terribly worried the whole time, and still not in touch with my feelings. Some people there came out with a lot of garbage, just because they didn't like you. By the end, I was totally confused – and even when I left, I still felt dreadful. But I think I needed Broadway Lodge.'

Broadway Lodge itself regards residential treatment as merely the first step to recovery: 'This is only the beginning in a very protected environment. The really hard work starts when they leave here,' according to one Broadway counsellor.

Waiting to help is an organization called Narcotics Anonymous, which uses the same principles as Broadway Lodge, making it possible for addicts to meet regularly and help each other, whether they have been through a treatment programme or not. Its advantage is that it costs nothing, and has no waiting-lists.

Hetty arrived back in London in April 1983, armed with instructions to go to Narcotics Anonymous meetings: 'I was having panic attacks the whole time, and was convinced I couldn't cope. But going to NA meetings every day helped a little bit. The first seven months weren't very good – but it got better slowly.'

She is not evangelical about the merits of Narcotics Anonymous, emphasizing that the groups have drawbacks in the same way as Broadway Lodge: 'It can be very narrow-minded and dogmatic – there's always outrage if you suggest there's any other way to give up. And sometimes the meetings are a bit like a cocktail party. But it has helped a lot of people including me. I don't know why – perhaps when you're an addict, you're lonely and friendless, and at least if you go to NA you see people who have given up, who are happy. As people talk about their experiences, you can identify with them. It's a great relief to find out that you're not alone, and that other people have got better. It gives you a sense of reality.'

Her story is repeated again and again at NA meetings. Annabel, a former model, started using heroin when she was 16, just after leaving boarding school: 'It was my crutch. I felt I was wrapped up in cotton wool. Nobody could hurt me. But things got out of hand very quickly. I tried the endless round of institutions and health-farms and acupuncturists. I tried to give up for five years before I started the NA programme. I didn't really want to go, but when I was at a meeting, I knew there was an answer – because I could see people there who had been addicts, who were now happy.'

This philosophy of mutual help has been extended to addicts' families through a sister organization, Families Anonymous, which has established over twenty groups throughout Britain. For people such as Sue, a 44-year-old teacher from Highgate, in north London, Families Anonymous has provided 'the only glimmer of hope' after she discovered her 19-year-old daughter was a heroin addict: 'By listening to other people's experiences, you begin to function at a reasonably tolerable level.'

Families Anonymous advises families to let addicts reach rock bottom, until they are forced to seek help themselves, and though Sue found the idea difficult to stomach, she believes the method works: 'Your natural instinct is to do something to help your child. But if you do, you prolong the time till they decide to go for treatment. You can't persuade, cajole or blackmail them – they have to decide for themselves.'

She also believes that mutual help works for people of all backgrounds, despite criticisms that FA and NA are predominantly middle-class organizations: 'At the Hampstead meetings I go to there are teachers, lecturers, tea-ladies, cleaners and small-business owners. Nobody cares about accent and class; what we have in common is that we care about our children.'

But FA and NA groups are by no means ubiquitous, and their approach does not suit everybody. They demand a certain amount of motivation and commitment which some addicts do not possess – and others simply may not like the intensive group sessions. One mother, who wrote to the *Sunday Times* about the difficulty of finding help for her young son, felt that these groups were second best to professional treatment: 'Parents without money are palmed off with Families Anonymous. It does not truly alleviate our misery to hear of the tribulations of others. My son is a talented artistic boy whose whole life will be ruined if he is not forcibly made to stop and rethink his life with a mind unclouded by drugs. By denying him properly supervised medical treatment, the state will probably incur more expense, exacting retribution from him, and long-term residence in a medical asylum for his mother.'

So although help groups like Families and Narcotics Anonymous cost nothing except for the considerable energy and time poured into them, they are not a cheap or final answer to the problems of treatment and rehabilitation.

There is no one 'correct' way to treat a heroin addict. Some users are able to give up at home, with the support of families and friends. One ex-addict, after a stay at Phoenix House of only two weeks, found his own ways of learning to live without heroin at home: 'A very important part in my rehabilitation has been filling the void left by drugs. In my case I began learning the violin and guitar – I still play them for pleasure and for therapy. I also strongly suspect that love, support and attention from one special person can play a big part in recovery.'

Other heroin addicts need the help of a hospital drugs clinic, or a friendly GP, or regular counselling from a local advice centre. Some need the long-term care of a residential rehabilitation house. But unfortunately many heroin addicts do not have this choice. David Turner, of SCODA, emphasizes that there are still gaping holes in the provision of treatment and rehabilitation: 'If you have a drugs problem, don't have it in Barnet or Bromley, or Cornwall or Devon. It would be unwise to have it in most of Derbyshire and Yorkshire. There are black spots all over the country.'

There is no instant solution to the problem of heroin addiction. It is not an illness that can be easily cured with a quick visit to the doctor and a course of medicine. Any answers demand hard work from the government, the health service, police, teachers, youth workers, parents – and addicts themselves. Heroin addiction is not going to quietly disappear. It is a problem that will stay in the community for a long time, and the whole community has to face up to its causes and devastating consequences.

The 'heroin epidemic' has been given a blaze of publicity by newspapers, television – and the government. So now that people have been made aware of the problem, some coherent strategies and solutions must be found. For, however much we might wish to forget the problem, the legacy of addiction will remain long after the glaring publicity fades away.

[7] *Help Guide*

Whilst every care has been taken in compiling the information contained in the appendix, which was correct at the time of going to press, the publishers cannot accept responsibility for any errors.

When an addict decides to give up heroin, the body may object when the drug is taken away. Withdrawal (or detoxification) usually starts eight to twenty-four hours after heroin was last taken – and the physical symptoms are like an attack of flu. The symptoms can include hot and cold sweats, nausea, vomiting, sleeplessness and runny eyes and noses. But the lurid picture of the agonies of 'cold turkey' is a magnification of the truth. The Community Drug Project, an advice service in south London, says: 'Heroin users, either because they genuinely believe the stories about the horrors of withdrawal, or because they really don't want to stop using and need an excuse, have a built-in interest in exaggerating how difficult it is to come off the drug. In fact, the pains of withdrawal from heroin, though unpleasant, are usually nothing like as bad as the mythology would have us believe.'

What is harder than the physical withdrawal from the drug is learning to live without it. Someone who has been using heroin for a long time may not be able to imagine life without the all-absorbing interest of the drug. They may have no other interests, and no friends who are not addicted to heroin. And stopping using the drug will not result in miraculous, fairy-tale changes in their lives. There will still be the problems of unemployment, or bad housing, or loneliness, or boredom, or insecurity – or any of the other things that led someone to heroin in the first place.

An addict has to come to terms with life without the comforting, cotton-wool effect of heroin – and this may demand a lot of help and support. Families and friends are sometimes able to provide this care, or it can come from a counsellor or a doctor. Sometimes a group of other ex-addicts can help – or a stay in a rehabilitation house.

Unfortunately, treatment facilities for heroin users are limited in many parts of the country. Those which do exist, particularly the voluntary organizations, may change or disappear. The main source of up-to-date information on where to get help is:

The Standing Conference on Drug Abuse (SCODA)
1–4 Hatton Place
Hatton Garden
London EC1N 8ND
tel (01) 430 2341

For those addicts who cannot or do not want to go to specialist drugs services, their local GP may be able to help. It is also worth remembering that most heroin users who decide to stop do so at home, with the help of family and friends. But the following lists give some idea of the services that are available.

Day Projects, Information and Advice Services

These services offer information and help to drug users, and some will give support and counselling to addicts and their families. The list is divided into regions to show people their nearest source of help.

Rehabilitation for drug users

This list gives information about residential rehabilitation projects. Almost all of them demand that someone going to a project should have given up using heroin – but this need only be a very short time before. They aim to help an addict stay off drugs, by under-standing why addiction took hold, and how to stop it happening again. They are all run by voluntary organizations, and usually expect referrals.

Blenheim Project, 7 Thorpe Close, London W10 5XL, tel (01) 960 5599: Advice, support, information and counselling for those with drug problems and their friends and families. The project also engages in educational work. Appointments necessary.

Cadett, 22 Lansdowne Road, London W11, tel (01) 727 9447: Advice, counselling and referral to other services.

Community Drug Advice Service, Oxlow Lane Clinic, Oxlow Lane, Dagenham, tel (01) 592 7748: Counselling and referral. Based in health centre, and helps with withdrawal for heroin users in the community.

Community Drug Project, 30 Manor Place, London SE17 3BB, tel (01) 703 0559: Counselling, referral, social-work support and prison visits for drug users in south London. Appointments preferred.

Drug Concern (Barnet), 1 Friern Park, North Finchley, London N12, tel (01) 445 5539: Advice and information for drug users and their families and friends.

Drugline, 28 Ballina St, Forest Hill, London SE23 1DR, tel (01) 291 2341: Support and advice for the parents of drug users.

Hungerford Drug Project, First floor, 26 Craven St, London WC2, tel (01) 930 4688: Advice, support, counselling and referral for those with drug problems. Drop in any time, or make an appointment (afternoons only). Hours: Monday and Wednesday, 2–5 pm; Tuesday, Thursday and Friday, 10 am–1 pm and 2 pm–5 pm.

Kaleidoscope Youth and Community Project, 40–46 Cromwell Road, Kingston-on-Thames, Surrey, tel (01) 549 2681/7488: Community centre providing counselling and recreational facilities for young people. Also has a medical surgery on Fridays. The centre has a hostel providing heroin support for young people (16–22). People should ring first for the opening hours of the various facilities.

Piccadilly Advice Centre, The Kiosk, Subway 4, Piccadilly Circus Underground, tel (01) 930 0066: General advice and information on the wide range of problems that may be faced by young people who have just arrived in London.

Portobello Project, 49–51 Porchester Road, London w2, tel (01) 221 4413/4425: Information/advice centre for young people in the local area, on drugs and other general information on accommodation, employment etc.

Substance Abuse Unit, 'Crossways', Whitehall Road, Uxbridge, Middlesex, tel Uxbridge 57285: Offers help in understanding drug abuse.

The Upstairs Project, 182 Hammersmith Road, London w6, tel (01) 741 3335: Centre offering advice and activities for young people (16–25) and counselling in an informal setting. (The centre is not just for drug users.)

2. THE SOUTH-EAST

Ashstead and Leatherhead APA, Arcades, 24 Oakfield Road, Ashstead, Surrey KT22 2RE, tel Ashstead 73979: Help and support for drug abusers and their families and friends. Regular group meetings and individual counselling.

Bridges, 9a–9b St Albans Road East, Hatfield, Herts, tel Hatfield 66834: Advisory, information and counselling service for young people (not a specialist service).

Herts and Beds Standing Conference on Drug Misuse, Room 1, Top floor, Danesbury Hospital, Welwyn, Herts, tel (043871) 6847: Advice, support and information for drug users, their families and friends.

Number 5, 2–4 Sackville St, Reading, Berks RG1 1NT, tel Reading 585858: General counselling and advice service, mainly for young people (though they will see older people). Will refer cases on to specialist agencies.

Southend Drug Advisory Service, tel South Benfleet (03745) 3121: Information and counselling service.

Stevenage Drugsline, Room 8, Family Centre, 13 Town Square, Stevenage SG1 1BP, tel (0438) 64067: Advice, support and information for drug users and their families and friends.

Surrey Drugline, tel Epsom 29266: A telephone advice and information service.

3. THE SOUTH-WEST

East Dorset Drugs Advisory Service, 79 Old Christchurch Road, Bourne-mouth BH1 1EW, tel (0202) 28718/28891: Advice and counselling service for people with drug problems and their families and friends. Ring first for an appointment.

4. WALES

Gwent Council on Alcoholism and Drug Addiction, Emlyn House, 3 Palmyra Place, Newport, Gwent, tel (0633) 63185: Counselling and advisory service for people with drug and alcohol problems.

South Wales APA, 111 Cowbridge Road East, Cardiff CF1 9AC, tel (0222) 26113: Counselling service, local education and talks.

5. THE MIDLANDS

Drugline, Dale House, New Meeting St, Birmingham 4, tel (021) 632 6363: Information and counselling for drug users, their families and friends. Counselling is given on the telephone, or by appointment.

6. THE NORTH-EAST

The Bridge Project, Equity Chambers, 40 Piccadilly, Bradford BD1 3NN, tel (0274) 723863: Counselling and advice for drug users, their families and friends. Also provides information and training for teachers, youth-workers and students.

Drugline (Sheffield), 302 Abbeydale Road, Sheffield 7, tel (0742) 558200: Counselling and advice for drug users, their families and friends. Telephone counselling, or interview by appointment.

7. THE NORTH-WEST

Lifeline Project Joddrell St, Manchester M3 3HE, tel (061) 832 6353: Information and advice service; day-centre facilities; assessment and referral for rehabilitation houses; advice and training for professionals and organizations.

Merseyside Drugs Council, 25 Hope St, Liverpool L1 9BQ, tel (051) 709 0074; or at the Wirral office: 3rd floor, Argyle Buildings, 69–71, Argyle St, Birkenhead L41 6AE: Information, advice counselling and educational programme.

8. SCOTLAND

Lothian Region

Drugs and Narcotics Anonymous, Simpson House, 52 Queen St, Edinburgh, tel (031) 225 6028: Based at the Church of Scotland's Family Counselling Centre. Offers mutual support and counselling, and a day-centre.

Leith Group, tel (031) 554 7516: A local group, based in Leith, offers help for drug users and their families. There is a resource and information library open to the public.

Support Help and Advice on Drug Addiction (SHADA), Unit 15, Muirhouse Shopping Centre, Muirhouse, tel (031) 332 2314: A local self-help group based in Muirhouse, Edinburgh.

Wester Hailes Hotline Project, tel (031) 442 2465: Information, advice and counselling service.

Strathclyde Region

Information and Resource Unit on Addiction, 82 West Regent St, Glasgow G2, tel (041) 332 0062: Information about advice and counselling services in Strathclyde.

Alban House, Cavendish St, Gorbals, Glasgow, tel (041) 429 7744: Counselling service and day centre.

Denmark St Day Project, Denmark St Health Centre, Denmark St, Possil, Glasgow G22, tel (041) 336 3365/4135: Information, advice and counselling for drug users and their families. No restriction on referrals.

Drugs Information Service, tel (041) 332 0063: Telephone information service.

Drugline, Allander St, Possilpark, Glasgow, tel (041) 336 3316: Support and counselling for drug users and their families.

Easterhouse Committee on Drug Abuse, tel (041) 773 2001: A local project providing advice, counselling and information.

North Pollock Addiction Centre, tel (041) 883 2222: Counselling, advice and information.

The Place, Possilpark, St Matthew's Rectory, 200 Balmore Road, Glasgow, tel (041) 336 8147: This non-denominational centre offers an in-patient detoxification unit, a twenty-four-hour drug-line, and a parents' support group, as well as information, advice and counselling. It takes people from all over Strathclyde.

Rainbow House, 1 Belhaven Terrace, Glasgow, tel (041) 339 2691: Day rehabilitation centre, open seven days a week.

St Enoch Centre, 13 South Portland St, Glasgow G5, tel (041) 429 5342: Day-facility for drug users, with counsellors and skill instructors.

The Tom Allan Centre, 23 Elmbank St, Glasgow G2 3PD, tel (041) 221 1535: Counselling service.

9. NATIONAL

Narcotics Anonymous, PO Box 246, c/o 47 Milman St, London SW10, tel (01) 351 6794: NA runs self-help groups for drug users – ring for details of times and places.

Families Anonymous, 88 Caledonian Road, London N1, tel (01) 278 8805: FA runs advice and support groups for families and friends of addicts.

1. GENERAL HOUSES

Alwin House, 40 Colville Terrace, London W11, tel (01) 229 0311 (Age: 18–24): The house will take young women and men, but they have to go there voluntarily.

Bridge House, Equity Chambers, 40 Piccadilly, Bradford 1, tel (0274) 723863 (Age: 16+): The house takes women and men who need some time to work out what to do after withdrawing from drugs. It will take people on bail, and on conditions of bail. Referrals should be made through the above address.

Cranstoun Project, 5 Ember Lane, Esher, Surrey, tel (01) 398 6956 (Age: 20–32): A community for men, run on democratic lines, and offering group and individual counselling.

Oak Lodge, 136 West Hill, London SW15, tel (01) 788 1648 (Age: 18–38): Community for men and women, with compulsory group sessions. Medical withdrawal can be arranged. Run on democratic lines.

Elizabeth House, 94 Redcliffe Gardens, London SW10, tel (01) 370 1279 (Age: 24–34): Long-term accommodation for men and women, with support group. Voluntary referrals only.

235 Project, 235 Balham High Road, London SW17, tel (01) 672 9464: A mixed hostel for ex-prisoners and ex-addicts.

2. CONCEPT HOUSES

The concept-rehabilitation houses require residents to work their way up a hierarchical structure and take part in very intensive group sessions. They are all mixed, taking men and women.

Alpha House, Wickham Road, Droxford, Southampton SO3 1PD, tel (0489) 877210 (Age: 16–42).

Inward House, 89 King St, Lancaster LA1 1RM, tel (0524) 69599 (Age: 16+.)

Ley Community, Sandy Croft, Sandy Lane, Yarnton, Oxford, tel (08675) 71777.

Phoenix House, 1 Eliot Bank, Forest Hill, London SE23, tel (01) 699 5748/1515.

Phoenix House Sheffield, 229 Graham Road, Ranmoor, Sheffield S10 3GS, tel (0742) 308 230/391.

Phoenix House South Shields, Westoe Drive, South Shields, Tyne and Wear NE33 3EW, tel (0632) 545544.

Suffolk House, Long Bridge, Slough Road, Iver Heath, Bucks, tel (0895) 56449 (Age: 17+.)

3. CHRISTIAN PHILOSOPHY HOUSES

These all expect a resident to accept a Christian approach, and believe in it in order to recover.

Chatterton Hey, Referrals to be made through: Keith Best, Langley House Trust, 26 Heaton Grove, Bradford BD9 4DY, tel (0274) 496838 (Age: 21–40. Men only.)

Deliverance International, 83 Aldersbrook Road, London E12, tel (01) 989 4610 (Men only.)

Life for the World Trust, Oldbury House, Oldbury Court Road, Fishponds, Bristol, tel (0272) 655582 (Age: 18–30. Men only.)

Meta House, 133 Princess Road, Westbourne, Bournemouth, tel (0202) 764581 (Age: 15–35): Women only, must be drug-free for two weeks before admission. Residents may stay up to three months.

Pye Barn Trust, 16 The Chase, London SW4, tel (01) 622 4870 (Age: 18–30. Men only.)

Yeldall Manor, Hare Hatch, near Twyford, Reading, Berks, tel (073 522) 2287 (Age: 18–31. Men only.)

4. HOUSES WITH CHRISTIAN STAFF

Coke Hole Trust, 70 Junction Road, Andover, Hants, tel (0264) 61045 (Age: 16–30. Men and women.)

Stillwaters, Nevendon Road, Nevendon, Basildon, Essex, tel (0268) 726357 (Age: 17–35. Men and women.) Run as an extended family home.

5. CRISIS CENTRE FOR DRUG USERS

City Roads Crisis Intervention Centre, 356/358 City Road, London EC1, tel (01) 278 8671 (Age: 17–30. Men and women.) Short stay (three weeks) to help drug users through withdrawal, when they have reached a crisis.

Private Clinics

Broadway Lodge, Oldmixon Road, Weston-Super-Mare, Avon BS24 9NN, tel (0934) 812319: Fees £665 a week (Broadway Lodge also offers 30 per cent of its places as assisted places). Broadway Lodge offers a short withdrawal programme, followed by counselling and group sessions.

The Priory, Priory Lane, London SW15, tel (01) 876 8261: Fees £145 a day. The Priory is a general psychiatric hospital, but it does have places for a few heroin addicts. It offers withdrawal, plus a short stay (about three weeks) with counselling.

Broadreach House, 465 Tavistock Road, Plymouth, tel (0752) 774275: Run on a charitable basis, with some assisted places and some fee-paying.

Hospitals

This list includes all the clinics that offer some form of treatment for drug addiction. Most of them operate a strict catchment area and have a waiting-list. Usually new patients have to be referred by their GPs. The treatment offered by these hospitals varies considerably. Some offer only outpatient therapy, others offer a bed where the addict can withdraw from heroin under medical supervision. Some clinics will prescribe drugs for addicts for varying periods; others refuse to prescribe drugs and rely on counselling methods.

(Note: The information that follows is as complete as was possible at the time of going to press. That for English and Welsh hospitals was supplied by the Standing Conference on Drug Abuse, that for Scottish hospitals by the Scottish Health Education Group.)

I. LONDON

a) *North-West Thames Health Region*

Charing Cross Hospital, Drug Dependency Unit, 57 Aspenlea Road, London w6, tel (01) 385 8834, Dr Oppenheim

St Bernard's Hospital, Drug Dependency Unit, Uxbridge Road, Southall (In-and Out-patient) tel (01) 843 0736, Dr D. H. Marjot

St Mary's Hospital, Drug Dependency Centre, Woodfield Road, London w9 (Out-patient) tel (01) 286 7371/2, Dr S. Das Gupta

West Middlesex Hospital, Drug Dependency Unit, Twickenham Road, Isleworth TW7 6AF, tel (01) 560 2121, Dr Curry

Westminster Drug Treatment Unit, 52–53 Vincent Square, London SW1 (Out-patient) tel (01) 828 9811 x397, Dr Pamela Aylett

b) *North-East Thames Health Region*

Hackney Hospital, Drug Dependency Unit, Homerton High Street, London E9 (Out-patient) tel (01) 986 6816, Dr J. W. Mack

The London Hospital, (St Clements), Drug Dependency Unit, 2a Bow Road, London E3 (Out-patient) tel (01) 980 4899 x237 or 981 3266, Dr John Cookson

University College Hospital, Drug Dependency Clinic, 122 Hampstead Road, London NW1 2LT (Out-patient) tel (01) 387 9300 x452/3/5, Dr Martin Mitcheson

c) *South-East Thames Health Region*

The Maudsley Hospital, Drug Unit, Denmark Hill, London SE5 8AZ (Out-patient) tel (01) 703 6333, Dr P. H. Connell

St Giles' Hospital, Drug Dependency Clinic, St Giles Road, London SE5 (Out-patient) tel (01) 703 0898, Dr Judith Morgan

St Thomas' Hospital, Drug Clinic, Lambeth Palace Road, London SE1 (Out-patient) tel (01) 633 0720, Dr T. H. Bewley

Tooting Bec Hospital, Drug Dependency Unit, Tooting Bec Road, London SW17 (In-patient) tel (01) 672 9933, Dr Hamid Ghodse

d) *South-West Thames Health Region*

Queen Mary's Hospital, Drug Treatment Unit, Roehampton Lane, London SW15 (In- and out-patient) tel (01) 789 6611 x309, Dr P. Aylett

St George's Hospital, Drug Treatment Unit, Clare House, Blackshaw Road, London SW17 0QT (In- and out-patient) tel (01) 672 1255 x4098/99, Dr Hamid Ghodse

2. THE SOUTH-EAST

Hill End Hospital, Hill End Lane, St Albans, Herts AL4 6RB, tel (0727) 55555

Luton and Dunstable Hospital, Department of Psychiatry, Dunstable Road, Beds LU4 0DZ (In- and out-patient) tel (0582) 53211, Dr Betty Chester

Queen Elizabeth II Hospital, Howlands, Welwyn Garden City, Herts AL7 4HQ, tel (07073) 28111, Dr McClure

Runwell Hospital, Wickford, Essex SS11 7QE (In- and out-patient) tel (03744) 5555 x271, Dr Neal J. P. Killala

Bethlem Royal Hospital, Drug Dependency Unit, Monks Orchard Road, Beckenham, Kent BR3 3BX (In-patient; no catchment area for non-injecting addicts) tel (01) 777 6611, Dr P. H. Connell

Bexley Hospital, Ashdown Ward, Old Bexley Lane, Bexley, Kent DA5 2BW (In-patient; no real catchment area for detoxification) tel (0322) 526282, Dr Judith Morgan

Brighton Drug Dependency Service, Herbert Hone Clinic, 11 Buckingham Road, Brighton BNI 3LQ (In- and out-patient) tel (0273) 23395/29604, Dr A. G. Farrington

Kent and Canterbury Hospital, Psychiatric Out-Patient Clinic, Ethelbert Road, Canterbury CTI 3NG (In- and out-patient) tel (0227) 66877, Dr M. F. Hussain

Brookwood Hospital, Knaphill, Surrey (In- and out-patient) tel (04867) 4545, Dr Browne

Crawley Hospital, West Green Drive, Crawley, tel (0293) 27866, Dr Rathod

Henderson Hospital, 2 Homeland Drive, Sutton, Surrey SU2 5LY (In- and out-patient) tel (01) 661 1611, Dr J. S. Whiteley

Rees House Day Hospital, 214 Moreland Road, East Croydon CRO 6NA, tel (01) 654 8100, Dr Sathananthan

St Christopher's Day Hospital, Hurst Road, Horsham, West Sussex, tel (0403) 4367, Dr Rathod

Ley Clinic, Littlemore Hospital, Oxford, tel (0865) 45651, Dr Mandelbrote

St John's Hospital, Psychiatric Service, Stone, Aylesbury, Bucks HPI7 8PP (In- and out-patient) tel (0296) 748383, Drs. Crouch, Cundall Davies and Fieldsend

Addenbrookes Hospital, Department of Psychiatry, 2 Bene't Place, Lensfield Road, Cambridge CB2 IEL (In- and out-patient) tel (0223) 355671 x415, Dr D. J. Muller

West Norwich Hospital, The Yare Clinic, Bowthorpe Road, Norwich NR2 3UD, tel (0603) 28377 (In- and out-patient)

3. THE SOUTH-WEST

'Top Lodge', Glenside Hospital, 20A Blackberry Hill, Stapleton, Bristol BSI6 IDD (Out-patient) tel (0272) 653285, Dr R. W. K. Reeves

Cheltenham General Hospital, Psychiatric Unit, Sandford Road, Cheltenham, Gloucester GL53 7AN (In- and out-patient) tel (0242) 580344 or (0452) 67033 x235, Dr Jeffrey Marks

Moorhaven Hospital, Psychiatric Service, Bittaford, Ivybridge, South Devon PL21 0EX, tel (07554) 2411, Dr A. J. Poole

Royal South Hants Hospital, Drug Dependence Clinic, Fanshawe, Southampton S09 4PE (In- and out-patient) tel (0703) 34288, Dr Guy Edwards

St Anne's Hospital, Drug Addiction Clinic, Haven Road, Canford Cliffs, Poole, Dorset (In- and out-patient) tel (0202) 708881, Dr N. Choudry

St James' Hospital, Drug Advice and Treatment Centre, Locksway Road, Portsmouth, Hants PO4 8LF (In- and out-patient) tel (0705) 735211 x294 or (0705) 823159, Dr Philip M. Fleming

4. WALES

Llandrindod Wells Hospital, Hazels Clinic, Llandrindod Wells, Powys (Outpatient) tel (0597) 2951, Dr M. Hussion

St Cadoc's Hospital, Caerleon, Gwent (In- and out-patient) tel (0633) 421121, Drs. Bird, Hughes, Evans, Lowther, Parsons and Waheed

University Hospital of Wales, Heath Park, Cardiff CF4 4XW (Out-patient) tel (0222) 755944, Dr A. Kellam

Whitchurch Hospital, Addiction Treatment Unit, Whitchurch, Cardiff CF4 7XB, tel (0222) 62191, Dr Keen

5. THE MIDLANDS

Towers Hospital, Humberstone, Leicester LE5 0TD (In-patient) tel (0533) 767184

St Crispin's Hospital, Duston, Northampton NN5 6UN, tel (0604) 52323, Dr Wharton

All Saints' Hospital, Lodge Road, Birmingham B18 5SD, tel (021) 523 5151, Dr N. Imlah

The Crypt Agency, 21 Temple St, Wolverhampton (Out-patient) tel (0902) 714401, Hilde Fuller

Newton Hospital, Worcester (In- and out-patient) tel (0905) 353507, Dr Milner, Mr N. Mounsey (social worker)

St George's Hospital, Drug Clinic, Personality Disorder Unit, Milford Ward, Stafford ST1 3AG (In- and out-patient) tel (0785) 3411 x243, Dr E. L. Mateu

6. THE NORTH-EAST

Parkwood House, Alcohol and Drug Dependence Unit, St Nicholas' Hospital, Gosforth, Newcastle-upon-Tyne NE3 3XT, tel (0632) 850151, Dr Anthony Thorley

South Tees Health Authority, Psychological Service, 22 Belle Vue Grove, Grove Hill, Middlesbrough, Cleveland (Out-patient) tel (0642) 827638, Mr J. J. Kear

Leeds Addiction Unit, 40 Clarendon Road, Leeds LS2 9PJ (In- and out-patient) tel (0532) 456617, Dr Duncan Raistrick

St Mary's Hospital, Dean Road, Scarborough YO12 7SN (In- and out-patient) tel (0723) 376111, Dr R. Seymour-Shove

Waddiloves Hospital, Forensic Psychiatric Unit, 44 Queens Road, Bradford BD8 7BT(In- and out-patient) tel (0274) 497121, Dr P. J. W. Wood

Mapperley Hospital, Porchester Road, Nottingham NG3 6AA (In- and out-patient) tel (0602) 608144, Dr P. C. McLean

Northern General Hospital, Herries Road, Sheffield S5 7AU (In- and out-patient) tel (0742) 382121, Professor Seager

Royal Hallamshire Hospital, Glossop Road, Sheffield S10 2JF (In- and out-patient) tel (0742) 26484, Professor F. A. Jenner

Arrowe Park Hospital, Detoxification Unit, Arrowe Park Road, Upton, Birkenhead (Out-patient) tel (051) 678 5111, Dr D. H. Miller

Halton Drug Dependency Unit, The Rear, 39–41 Victoria Road, Widnes, Cheshire (Out-patient, part-time service) tel (051) 423 5247, Coordinator: Mike Ryan

Hope Street Clinic, 30 Hope Street, Liverpool (Out-patient) tel (051) 709 0516, Dr Marks

Moston Hospital, Upton by Chester, Chester CH2 4AA, tel (0244) 25202, Dr Madden

Parkside Hospital, Victoria Road, Macclesfield, Mersey (Out-patient, nominal service) tel (0625) 21000

Sefton General Hospital, Smithdown Road, Liverpool L15 2HE, tel (051) 733 4020

St Helen's Hospital, Psychiatric Out-Patient, Marshalls Cross Road, St Helen's, Merseyside WA9 3EA (Out-patient) tel (0744) 26633, Dr R. L. Duncan

West Cheshire Hospital, Mersey Regional DDU, Liverpool Road, Chester (Out-patient) tel (0244) 379333 x314 or 315500 x402, Dr J. S. Madden

Winwick Hospital, Winwick Addiction Unit, Winwick, Lancs. (In-patient) tel (0925) 55211, Dr John Marks

Birch Hill Hospital, Psychiatric Dept, Rochdale, Lancs. OL12 9QB (In- and out-patient) tel (0706) 77777

Prestwich Hospital, Prestwich, Manchester M25 7BL, tel (061) 773 2236 x11, Dr J. Strang

Dumfries

Crichton Royal Hospital, Glencairn Unit, Dumfries DG1 4TG (In- and out-patient) tel (0387) 55301, Dr Kennedy

Dundee

Royal Dundee Liff Hospital, Dundee Psychiatric Service, Liff by Dundee DD2 5NF (In- and out-patient) tel (0382) 580441, Dr B. Johnstone

Edinburgh

Royal Edinburgh Hospital, Andrew Duncan Clinic, Morningside Terrace, Edinburgh EH10 5HF tel (031) 447 2011, Dr John Basson

Glasgow

Duke Street Hospital, Carswell House, 5 Oakley Terrace, Glasgow G31 2HX (In- and out-patient) tel (041) 554 6267, Dr R. N. Antebi

Gartnavel General Hospital, Ward 1A, 1053 Great Western Road, Glasgow, tel (041) 334 8122, Dr MacDonald

Leverndale Hospital, Crookston Road, Glasgow (In- and out-patient) tel (041) 882 6255, Dr J. K. Binns,

Southern General Hospital, Drug Clinic, Gowan Road, Glasgow G51 4TF (In- and out-patient) tel (041) 445 2466 x3300 or 332 5463, Dr P. J. Mullin

Woodilee Hospital, Alcohol/Drug Unit, Lenzie, Glasgow G66 (In- and out-patient) tel (041) 776 2451, Dr M. Z. Rahman

Borders Region

Peel Hospital, Galashiels TD1 3LQ, tel (0896) 2295

Dingleton Hospital, Mental Health Service, Melrose, Roxburghshire TD6 9HN (In- and out-patient) tel (089682) 2727, Dr D. M. H. Jones

Bellsdyke Hospital, Larbert, tel (0324) 56131

Fife Region

Stratheden Hospital, Springfield, Cupar KY15 5RR, tel (0334) 2611

Grampian Region

Royal Cornhill Hospital, Cornhill Road, Aberdeen AB9 2ZH, tel (0224) 52411

Bilbohall Hospital, 34 Pluscarden Road, Elgin LV30 1SL, tel (0343) 3131

Kingseat Hospital, Newmachar, Aberdeenshire AB5 0NH, tel (065) 17253

Highland Region

Craig Dunain Hospital, Inverness IV3 6JU, tel (0463) 234101

Northern Ireland

Shaftesbury Square Hospital, 116–118 Great Victoria Street, Belfast BT2 7BG, tel (0232) 29808

Appendix: The opium wars

Britain's involvement in opium traffic, a period which Brian Inglis in his book *The Forbidden Game* calls 'the most protractedly sordid episode in British imperial history', began when Clive of India defeated the French at Plassey in 1757 and inherited the Moghul Empire in Bengal.

The British East India Company also inherited the Moghuls' monopoly of the opium trade. Before Plassey, the Company had to buy the opium from Bengal and take it to China. Now the Company sold its Indian opium to merchant-ship owners who would smuggle it into China for them. But it had effective control over every aspect of the chain of distribution, much as today's top heroin traffickers exercise their control – all along the line.

In 1772, when Warren Hastings became Governor-General of British India, he described opium as a 'pernicious commodity' but immediately set about expanding the trade with China, using privateers or 'country ships'. His motives were those of the classic drug trafficker – the drug's potential for generating huge profits.

The British opium trade in the East in the nineteenth century and the addiction crisis it caused in China mirrored the heroin epidemic in Britain today caused by Asian heroin. It was the first time that opium was treated as an international commodity to be marketed on a vast scale. The debate which waged in China between the champions of prohibition and those who urged legalization of the drug as a solution is repeated in today's debate between the American method of 'law enforcement' to crack down on heroin traffic and the traditional UK response of giving addicts heroin or its substitutes to keep them stable and quell the black market.

China became increasingly concerned. It had used opium medicinally for a long time but, in the seventeenth century, the Emperor discovered that some of his subjects had started a new fad – they were burning small quantities of opium in the flame of a candle and inhaling the fumes (the traditional chasing-the-dragon technique, which has now hit Britain). He tried to ban the new pastime but the number of users spread slowly with opium supplied first by the Portuguese.

However it was when the British entered the trade that China's problems mushroomed. The Emperor issued edicts, pleadings, warnings and threats against opium. The 'country ships' licensed by the British East India Company simply extended their activities. By 1813, opium had reached Peking and members of the Chinese court as well as 'vagabonds' were addicted. The British promised several times to keep production down. But, by the 1820s, four times more Indian opium was reaching China at lower prices than ten years before.

In 1830 the British Parliament decided to investigate the East India Company's opium trade, but recommended that it would not be desirable to 'abandon so important a source of revenue'. The value of exports of opium to China for the British was now over £2 million. The British government was now directly responsible for opium traffic but this did not lead to a more restrained approach.

Forty thousand chests of opium were sent to China in 1839. There were now addicts in the Chinese army, stories of opium smuggled from Canton to Peking in the diplomatic bag and the increasing involvement of officials, merchants and civil servants who were subject to blackmail and extortion. Thoughtful Chinese academics sent memos to the Emperor suggesting that opium should be legalized: prohibition was not only failing to control the drug's spread but created its own social evils – corruption and violence.

But the Emperor's more hard-headed advisors disagreed and fervently advocated a crack-down on the opium sellers who lived in Canton – the sellers were to be arrested, ships to be sent back and all trade embargoed until the opium smuggling stopped. But at the slightest whiff of suppression of the trade, the British sent an expeditionary force to punish the Chinese and to restore 'free trade'.

This led to the First Opium War (1839–1842), which the Chinese lost.

The British now began a campaign to persuade the Chinese to make opium commerce legal 'in their own interest'. Regardless, the Emperor issued fresh edicts against smoking with draconian measures to stamp it out, but the rise in addicts and the opium available was unrelenting. The escalating tension led to the Second Opium War of 1856.

The British won again and this time forced the Emperor to legalize opium. But legalization proved no more effective than prohibition in suppressing the trade. Supply and demand both rapidly increased and in twenty years the number of chests coming to China almost doubled from under 60,000 chests in 1859 to 105,000 in 1879.

Back in Britain the anti-opium feelings of the 1840s were fanned with the foundation of the Oriental Society for the Suppression of Opium which demanded that the government should give up its opium monopoly in India and stop pushing the drug in China. The public heard conflicting reports of the opium trade. Sir Thomas Wade, a British negotiator with China, said of the wars, 'The concessions made to us have been from the first to the last extorted against the conscience of the nation ... opium has led to the steady descent, moral and physical, of the smoker.'

But Jardine Mathieson, an opium merchant, wrote to the governor of Hong Kong (which Britain won from the Chinese after the First Opium War) in 1867: 'It has been rendered abundantly clear that the use of opium is not a curse but a comfort and a benefit to the hard-working Chinese.' Jardine Mathieson is still a major Hong-Kong international trading company with property and insurance interests to this day.

The opium trade carried on more or less unabated for the rest of the nineteenth century. But, by the 1890s, opium was a declining proportion of the Indian budget and domestic pressure to end the trade was growing. The Liberal government which returned to power in 1906 began negotiations and in 1908 agreed to reduce opium exports from India to China. The trade was eventually stamped out by a series of international measures to crack down on drug trafficking.

MORE ABOUT PENGUINS, PELICANS
AND PUFFINS

For further information about books available from Penguins please write to Dept EP, Penguin Books Ltd, Harmondsworth, Middlesex UB7 0DA.

In the U.S.A.: For a complete list of books available from Penguins in the United States write to Dept DG, Penguin Books, 299 Murray Hill Parkway, East Rutherford, New Jersey 07073.

In Canada: For a complete list of books available from Penguins in Canada write to Penguin Books Canada Ltd, 2801 John Street, Markham, Ontario L3R 1B4.

In Australia: For a complete list of books available from Penguins in Australia write to the Marketing Department, Penguin Books Australia Ltd, P.O. Box 257, Ringwood, Victoria 3134.

In New Zealand: For a complete list of books available from Penguins in New Zealand write to the Marketing Department, Penguin Books (N.Z.) Ltd, Private Bag, Takapuna, Auckland 9.

In India: For a complete list of books available from Penguins in India write to Penguin Overseas Ltd, 706 Eros Apartments, 56 Nehru Place, New Delhi 110019.

THE PENGUIN ENGLISH DICTIONARY

The Penguin English Dictionary has been created specially for today's needs. It features:

* More entries than any other popularly priced dictionary
* Exceptionally clear and precise definitions
* For the first time in an equivalent dictionary, the internationally recognised IPA pronunciation system
* Emphasis on contemporary usage
* Extended coverage of both the spoken and the written word
* Scientific tables
* Technical words
* Informal and colloquial expressions
* Vocabulary most widely used *wherever* English is spoken
* Most commonly used abbreviations

It is twenty years since the publication of the last English dictionary by Penguin and the compilation of this entirely new *Penguin English Dictionary* is the result of a special collaboration between Longman, one of the world's leading dictionary publishers, and Penguin Books. The material is based entirely on the database of the acclaimed *Longman Dictionary of the English Language.*

1008 pages   051.139 3   £2.50   □

PENGUIN REFERENCE BOOKS

☐ *The Penguin Map of the World* £2.50

Clear, colourful, crammed with information and fully up-to-date, this is a useful map to stick on your wall at home, at school or in the office.

☐ *The Penguin Map of Europe* £2.95

Covers all land eastwards to the Urals, southwards to North Africa and up to Syria, Iraq and Iran * Scale = 1:5,500,000 * 4-colour artwork * Features main roads, railways, oil and gas pipelines, plus extra information including national flags, currencies and populations.

☐ *The Penguin Map of the British Isles* £1.95

Including the Orkneys, the Shetlands, the Channel Islands and much of Normandy, this excellent map is ideal for planning routes and touring holidays, or as a study aid.

☐ *The Penguin Dictionary of Quotations* £3.95

A treasure-trove of over 12,000 new gems and old favourites, from Aesop and Matthew Arnold to Xenophon and Zola.

☐ *The Penguin Dictionary of Art and Artists* £3.95

Fifth Edition. 'A vast amount of information intelligently presented, carefully detailed, abreast of current thought and scholarship and easy to read' – *The Times Literary Supplement*

☐ *The Penguin Pocket Thesaurus* £1.95

A pocket-sized version of Roget's classic, and an essential companion for all commuters, crossword addicts, students, journalists and the stuck-for-words.

PENGUIN REFERENCE BOOKS

☐ **The Penguin Dictionary of Troublesome Words**   £2.50

A witty, straightforward guide to the pitfalls and hotly disputed issues in standard written English, illustrated with examples and including a glossary of grammatical terms and an appendix on punctuation.

☐ **The Penguin Guide to the Law**   £7.50

This acclaimed reference book is designed for everyday use, and forms the most comprehensive handbook ever published on the law as it affects the individual.

☐ **The Penguin Dictionary of Religions**   £4.95

The rites, beliefs, gods and holy books of all the major religions throughout the world are covered in this book, which is illustrated with charts, maps and line drawings.

☐ **The Penguin Medical Encyclopedia**   £4.95

Covers the body and mind in sickness and in health, including drugs, surgery, history, institutions, medical vocabulary and many other aspects. Second Edition. 'Highly commendable' – *Journal of the Institute of Health Education*

☐ **The Penguin Dictionary of Physical Geography**   £4.95

This book discusses all the main terms used, in over 5,000 entries illustrated with diagrams and meticulously cross-referenced.

☐ **Roget's Thesaurus**   £2.95

Specially adapted for Penguins, Sue Lloyd's acclaimed new version of Roget's original will help you find the right words for your purposes. 'As normal a part of an intelligent household's library as the Bible, Shakespeare or a dictionary' – *Daily Telegraph*

A CHOICE OF
PELICANS AND PEREGRINES